W9-BOL-504

THE ASSAULT

Also by Brian Falkner

The Tomorrow Code

Brain Jack

The Project

THE ASSAULT

BRIAN FALKNER

Random House New York

 Published in the United States by Random House Children's Books, a division of Random House, Inc., New York. Originally published in paperback in Australia and New Zealand by Walker Books Australia, Newtown, in 2011.

Random House and the colophon are registered trademarks of Random House, Inc.

Symbol art by snoopydoo

Visit us on the Web! randomhouse.com/teens

Educators and librarians, for a variety of teaching tools, visit us at RHTeachersLibrarians.com

Library of Congress Cataloging-in-Publication Data
Falkner, Brian.
The assault / Brian Falkner. — 1st American ed.
p. cm.
Summary: In the year 2030, six teens who have been modified to look like the aliens who are battling for control of Earth go behind enemy lines and discover a shocking, secret alien project.
ISBN 978-0-375-86946-4 (trade) — ISBN 978-0-375-96946-1 (lib. bdg.) — ISBN 978-0-375-98351-1 (ebook)
[1. Extraterrestrial beings—Fiction. 2. War—Fiction. 3. Undercover operations—Fiction. 4. Adventure and adventurers—Fiction. 5. Australia—Fiction. 6. Science fiction.] I. Title.
PZ7.F1947As 2012 [Fic]—dc23 2011042888

Printed in the United States of America
10 9 8 7 6 5 4 3 2 1
First American Edition

Random House Children's Books supports the First Amendment and celebrates the right to read.

For Henry
1964–2011
You were an inspiration.

▪ CONTENTS ▪

PROLOGUE

THIS IS NOT A HISTORY BOOK.

The achievements of 4th Reconnaissance Team (designation: Angel) of the Allied Combined Operations Group, 1st Reconnaissance Battalion, from November 2030 through July 2035, during the Great Bzadian War, are well documented by scholars and historians. Less well known are the people behind the myth: the brave young men and women who earned the reputation and the citations for which Team Angel became famous.

These are their stories, pieced together from Post-Action Reports and interviews with the surviving members of the team. The stories of the heroes whose skills, daring, and determination changed the course of history.

Where necessary, to gain a full understanding of the situations that these soldiers faced, accounts have been included from the forces they opposed: from interviews with prisoners and Bzadian reports of the battles.

The members of Recon Team Angel changed over time, due to injury and death, as you would expect in a combat arena. By the end of the war, over seventy young people had served in the unit. They were ages fourteen to eighteen—small enough to pass themselves off as alien soldiers but old enough to undertake high-risk covert operations behind enemy lines.

At its peak, this remarkable group boasted a core of twenty-five specialist operatives. But in the beginning there were only six:

Angel One: Lieutenant Ryan (Lucky) Chisnall—United States of America

Angel Two: Sergeant Holly Brogan—Australia

Angel Three: Specialist Stephen (Hunter) Huntington—United Kingdom

Angel Four: Specialist Janos (Monster) Panyoczki—Hungary

Angel Five: Private First Class Blake Wilton—Canada

Angel Six: Private First Class Trianne (Phantom) Price—New Zealand

May we always remember the names of those who fell in the pursuit of liberty for Earth.

BOOK I—RECON

1. WHERE ANGELS FEAR

[MISSION DAY 1]

[2335 hours local time]

[F-35 Lightning II Stealth Bomber, somewhere over the center of Australia]

"ANGEL CHARIOT, THIS IS HEAVEN. HOW COPY?"

"Heaven, this is Angel Chariot, clear copy, over."

"Angel Chariot, we have zero five bogies now airborne in your proximity. Repeat, zero five bogies. Expect enemy craft approaching from your six. Anticipate interception in one seven mikes, confirm."

"Angel Chariot confirming zero five bogies, interception in one seven mikes."

"Confirmation acknowledged, Angel Chariot. Proceed as planned. Good luck. Out."

The voices in his ear fell silent, and Lieutenant Ryan

Chisnall glanced around at the vague shadows that were the five other members of his team, crouched together in the impossibly small space in the bomb bay of the aircraft. A space that was not designed to hold human beings.

The other members of the team couldn't hear the voices of the pilot (snug in the cockpit somewhere above them) and their mission controller (safe thousands of miles away at the Operational Command Center). Only Chisnall had a link to this channel, so the others did not know that five enemy jets were heading their way and the first would be right on their tail in less than seventeen minutes.

He decided not to tell them.

A ripple of fear welled up from his gut, stretching dark fingers out around his chest. His heart began to race as a tingling sensation spread from his fingertips to his shoulders.

He took a deep breath and expelled it slowly, humming to himself as he did. Panic, not the circumstances, was the killer. That was what his combat instructor had rammed home again and again. Fear is your friend, keeping you sharp. But panic is the unclean spirit, twisting your soul, consuming logic, training, and, finally, you. So Chisnall hummed to himself and, in doing so, banished the panic to the far corners of his mind.

"Okay, final sys-checks," he said in a steady voice.

The noise inside the fuselage of the plane would have deafened a corpse. The bomb bay had been heated and pressurized for this mission, but not soundproofed. With the continuous roar from the other side of the bomb bay doors, it was like being in front of the speakers at a thrash metal concert. If they hadn't all been wearing comm units, talk would have been impossible.

One by one, each of the team members' systems checks came up on his HMDS. Five of them had sys-OK, including him, but one was showing a problem.

"Angel Three, you're showing a helmet breach. What's going on, Hunter?" Chisnall could barely see Specialist Stephen "Hunter" Huntington, although he was no more than a few feet away from him. The darkness in the fuselage was almost absolute. The only light came from the ready lights on the six half-pipes on the floor beneath their feet.

"Just scratchin' my nose, Angel One," Hunter replied, and his sys-check lit up before he finished speaking.

"Picking your nose, you mean," Private First Class Trianne Price said.

"This is Angel Five. I have visual confirmation, over," Private First Class Blake Wilton said. "He was definitely picking."

"Mate," Sergeant Holly Brogan said, "if Hunter could pick his nose, would he have picked that one?"

Hunter's voice came immediately in Chisnall's ear. "Angel One, I wish to report Sergeant Brogan for breach of regulations, subsection C, paragraph six—intentionally dischargin' a joke that's older than my grandmother, without regard for the safety of others."

"Is not Price your grandmother?" Specialist Janos "Monster" Panyoczki asked.

"Bite me," Price said, and there was a muffled thump on the comm.

Chisnall grinned. Nearly eighteen, "Phantom" Price was the oldest member of the team.

The pilot's voice cut across the banter. "Angel One, this is Angel Chariot, how copy?"

"Angel Chariot, this is Angel One. Clear copy," Chisnall replied immediately.

"Angel One, I have six greens showing on my board. Please confirm you are ready to Echo Victor."

"Angel One confirming six sys-OKs. All angels ready to fly, over."

"Echo Victor in approximately one four mikes, confirm?"

"Confirm Echo Victor in one four mikes." Chisnall checked his pulse again. Fourteen minutes until the EV, which was just a short way of saying they were going to be ejected from a fast-moving jet at 32,000 feet.

"Fourteen mikes! That's crap," Wilton said. "Let's go now. I can't wait to stick it down those Bzadian throats. Booyah!"

Chisnall thought he could hear a tremor in Wilton's voice, despite all his bravado.

"You know we can't," he said. "We have to wait until the pilot fires off chaff. As soon as one of the Pukes gets missile lock on us, we are out of here."

"So hit the chaff and let's go," Wilton said.

"Wilton, ya plonker," Hunter said. "If Angel Chariot releases chaff before one of the Pukes gets missile lock, then the Pukes start saying to themselves, 'What'd he do that for?' And the last thing we need is a bunch of suspicious Pukes on our six."

"Yeah, and if the Puke gets a shot off before we EV, then we're CFC!" Wilton said.

"CFC? What is this CFC?" Monster asked. "Not in the SMTPA manual."

"Crispy fried chicken," Holly Brogan informed him.

Chisnall shook his head. "If we don't jump in the chaff, then we might as well take out a front-page ad on Google, telling the Pukes we're on our way."

"I know it, LT," Wilton said. "But that don't make it any easier to sit up here with our butts hanging out waiting for the first Puke fast mover to kick us where it hurts."

"You think?" Price said.

Silence spread like a thick cloud through the confined space. This was it. The real thing. A combat drop over enemy territory. A first for all of them. Chisnall couldn't see their faces, but he could sense their tension.

The timing had to be perfect. A second wrong either way and the mission was compromised or they were dead. Which pretty much amounted to the same thing.

The Operational Command Center, with its all-seeing satellite eyes, was back on the comm to the pilot of their aircraft.

"Angel Chariot, this is Heaven. How copy?"

"Clear copy, Heaven."

"Interceptors passing through two zero kilo feet. Anticipate interception in zero eight mikes. Looks like type ones, over."

Intelligence had identified four different types of enemy fast movers since the start of the war. Type ones were smaller, lightly armed but faster. The first of them was already over 20,000 feet, on its way to blow Angel Chariot out of the sky in less than eight minutes.

Chisnall stretched his legs as much as he could in the confined space. His knees were jammed up against the hard plastic shell of his half-pipe. It had been triple-checked before takeoff, and the green ready light in the center of the case glowed dimly.

A minute passed, and another. Chisnall ticked them off on his HMDS. Three minutes, four minutes, five.

The pilot spoke again in his ear. "Angel One, this is Angel Chariot."

"Angel One receiving," Chisnall replied.

"Assume launch position. Confirm."

Chisnall looked at the vague shapes around him. "Okay, team, grab your bags, stick your heads between your legs, and get ready to kiss your butts goodbye."

There was a proper protocol for telling them they were about to launch, and that was not it. But protocol or not, they all reached down and grasped the handles on their half-pipes, rolling onto them and lying lengthwise to reduce the impact of the slipstream once they dropped.

"Angel Chariot, this is Angel One. Launch position confirmed, over."

"Stand by for pressurization."

"Standing by."

There was a hiss and his flight suit compacted slightly as the air pressure in the bay increased.

"I'm not getting paid enough for this," Wilton said.

"You're getting paid?" Brogan asked.

"Stand by. Stand by."

Chisnall gripped the handles on his half-pipe tightly. His pulse was racing, but there was no trace of panic. Not now. They had done this dozens of times in training and hundreds of times in the simulator. Reflexes took over. His mind was on autopilot, preparing for the sudden drop and the shocking blast of air.

Only seconds now.

"Angel Chariot, this is Heaven. We are seeing zero two bogies forming up in attack position on your six. How copy?"

"Clear copy. I see them, Heaven."

More seconds passed.

"What are they doing?" Wilton's words came through gritted teeth.

"Cut the chatter and prepare to Echo Victor," Chisnall said.

"Missile lock! Missile lock! Deploying chaff. Echo Victor. Echo Victor. Echo Victor."

One moment there was a solid floor beneath them, and the next, nothing.

The bomb bay doors slid away instantly, and the pressure inside blasted them from the aircraft in a kick of rushing air. They were out, the F-35 pulling up and to the right. Chisnall clung to his half-pipe, trying to meld himself with the device as they rode the angular, bomblike shapes out into the night sky.

The cold was immediate and shocking, like needles of ice all over his body, despite his thermal flight suit. His breath fogged his faceplate for a second before the suit's internal mechanisms took care of it. The slipstream tore at his helmet and the heavy leather of his flight gloves, trying to rip him from his half-pipe. Chaff cylinders were exploding around him as he fell through twirling spirals of metal that turned the sky to silver.

Six highly trained Special Forces soldiers falling through the night.

One air-cushioned equipment canister full of supplies.

Zero parachutes.

[2350 hours]

[Early Warning Radar Center, Uluru Military Base, New Bzadia]

The glow of the radar screen added its light to those of the others around the circumference of the room, casting a green haze over everything and everyone.

Inzusu's eyes were fixed on a dot on the screen. Just a few glowing pixels, but at that moment every cell in his body was focused on them. A human jet, invading Bzadian airspace. The first he had seen in almost two years of radar duty.

It was beyond reason that the scumbugz, the *humans,* on the verge of being wiped from the face of the planet, would dare to send an aircraft here, to the heart of New Bzadia.

"You're sure there's just one intruder?" Czali, his supervisor, leaned over his shoulder.

Inzusu rotated the three-dimensional display around to the horizontal.

"There's just a single return, and if there were two of them, there would have to be some horizontal or vertical separation. I'm sure it's a single plane."

"Makes no sense," Czali murmured. "It's not an attack, and they don't need recon; they have satellites to do that."

Every move they made on this god-forgotten planet was closely watched by the satellite eyes of the natives.

"By Azoh!" Inzusu said as a bright flare appeared where the dot had been.

"It's just chaff," Czali said. "Where are our interceptors?"

Inzusu pointed at a group of red dots on the screen, each marked with a number and a call sign. "We already have missile lock. The chaff won't help them."

Czali made a murmuring sound of agreement.

"What's this?" Inzusu asked, pointing at a faint flicker on the screen.

Czali leaned forward. Inzusu rotated the display up and down, trying different angles and zooming in. Whatever it was, it was dropping from the chaff cloud, just the faintest of ghostly echoes.

"Empty chaff canister?" Czali suggested.

"There's another one," Inzusu said. "Parachutes? Have the scumbugz pilots bailed out?"

Czali shook her head. "Parachutes give a much bigger return, and these are falling, not floating. Just debris, I think, but keep an eye on them."

"We're firing," Inzusu said, forgetting the ghosts. He watched with excitement as two tiny dots detached from one of the interceptors and streaked toward the intruder.

Three seconds into the fall, Chisnall thrust the half-pipe away and starfished, the webbing between his arms and legs grabbing at the air and slowing his fall. Not much, but enough. His half-pipe, sleek and angular, continued to fall, disappearing below him.

He was through the chaff cloud now and encased in a dark blanket of night. Below him, Australia, the great desert, stretched on forever. Only a faint thumbprint of city light far to the south interrupted the vast emptiness. Somewhere near him were the five phantoms that were his team members, black shapes in a black sky over a black land.

"Missile launch. Missile launch. Deploying flares, breaking high and right." The pilot sounded impossibly calm in the sky above their heads.

Chisnall did not respond. There was nothing to say.

The enemy radar systems were highly sophisticated, much

more advanced than their own. But the small half-pipe dropping away somewhere below him was the ultimate in stealth technology: all flat surfaces and plasma screening and a built-in radar detection system that would activate small fins on the casing and turn the half-pipe away from any radar sources. At night, it was all but invisible. Likewise, his stealth flight suit would automatically orient itself to present the lowest possible radar profile to the enemy.

The battle above their heads was intensifying. The type ones, the enemy craft, were faster and more agile than even the best human aircraft, and Angel Chariot had no way to evade them.

But hiding in the sky was a surprise for the Pukes.

"Multiple signals!" Inzusu screamed. A swarm of dots had suddenly appeared on his screen. He stabbed at the comms button. "Multiple signals, right behind you. Immediate evasive maneuvers!"

The pilots of the interceptors reacted immediately, breaking formation and streaking into different parts of the sky.

"Where in Azoh's name did they come from?" Czali asked behind him, an accusatory tone in her voice.

"Out of nowhere."

"They're not aircraft; they're missiles, hunter-seekers," Czali said, examining the screen.

"Hunter-seekers? The scumbugz don't have hunter-seekers!"

"They do now. Must have got hold of one of ours and reverse-engineered it."

"Azoh!" Inzusu hit the comms button again. "Get out of there, now! Multiple hunter-seeker missiles right behind you. Repeat, multiple hunter-seekers right on your tails."

Already, the tiny hunter-seekers were accelerating to attack speed and targeting the closest interceptor. He could imagine the shock on the pilots' faces as they suddenly realized the danger behind them and broke off the attack on the scumbugz to fight for their own lives. Their planes had sophisticated antimissile systems, but the enemy missiles were hunting in packs.

Czali swore as two of the red dots blinked, then disappeared from the screen.

Two more flashes lit the sky above Chisnall, fading into the distance as he fell.

"Heaven, this is Angel Chariot. I have two confirmed hunter-seeker kills. How copy?"

"Clear copy, Angel Chariot. Confirming two kills, over." The pilot continued dispassionately. *"I have three-way missile lock. I am breaking low and left, heading for home."* Then his voice changed. *"Missile launch! Missile launch! I have multiple inbound missiles. Confirming zero six missiles, over."*

Chisnall's heart sank. The remaining enemy craft had closed within range. There were six air-to-air missiles swarming toward Angel Chariot.

The second wave of hunter-seekers hit their targets with three explosions and three blasts of light. That was the last of them, but it was too late.

The voice of the pilot was back in his ear in quick, unemotional sentences. *"Countermeasures deployed. Missiles are closing. Going for the moon, over."*

The pilot had tipped his jet back and was now rocketing skyward, vertically, like a rocket lifting off, hoping to leave the missiles below him. But it was not going to work. It was never going to work.

"Missiles still closing. Missiles—"

There was another boom.

Chisnall cursed under his breath.

Angel Chariot was now fragments of metal and exploding fuel tanks, a fiery meteor falling back to Earth. But it had played its part. It had given the enemy radar something to focus on, a distraction, as the six angels fell toward the desert floor below.

There was silence as the last of the red dots blinked and faded from the screen. Inzusu gritted his teeth. They were not just dots. They were comrades. Bzadians. Killed by the scumbugz that infested this planet.

"We need to wipe this planet clean," he said.

"Disinfect it," Czali agreed grimly.

Inzusu turned his attention back to the ghostly echoes fading in and out on his radar screen. Still no sign of parachutes. The echoes were falling like stones. Just to be sure, he kept watching until the faint signals crashed to the sand of the New Bzadian desert.

Chisnall continued flaring his arms and legs. Already the others would be accelerating down away from him. It was standard operating procedure to stagger the landings, for safety reasons. He would be the last of his team to land so if things went wrong, he would have a few more seconds to figure out what to do, although in reality that probably just meant a few seconds longer to live.

He checked his timing, tucked his arms and legs into his body, and felt the acceleration as he dropped faster and faster. Already he was falling as fast as a human being could fall: terminal velocity.

"Angel Six down, all Oscar Kilo." Price—the first to land—sounded winded, but that was normal for this type of jump.

"Angel Five down. Oscar Kilo, Oscar Kilo." Wilton was also down and okay.

Chisnall's eyes were glued to his HMDS, waiting for the signal from his own half-pipe. There it was: a yellow light and a *pip, pip* alert in his ear. His half-pipe was due to impact in three, two, one . . . The *pip*-ing stopped. There was a moment's silence, followed by a screech inside his helmet and a red flashing light.

The half-pipe had failed to deploy.

He punched at the manual override. Another screech, and the red light was still blasting at him. His landing gear had failed.

Those panicky hands were back around his heart and nothing was going to persuade them to loosen their grip. Lieutenant Ryan Chisnall of the Allied Combined Operations Group, Reconnaissance Battalion, was now falling toward the barren Australian desert at terminal velocity.

Very terminal.

2. TERMINAL VELOCITY

THE HIGH-ALTITUDE FREE-FALL LANDING PAD—PERSONNEL (HAFLP-P) was developed in secret by the British military in the early 2010s. Designed as a clandestine insertion method, it was regarded as so secret by the British that not even their U.S. allies were privy to the project. Not until the Bzadian War, at least. After that, countries keeping secrets from each other seemed pointless, as human forces allied against the alien intruders.

The HAFLP-P, commonly known as the "half-pipe," worked off a basic law of physics: terminal velocity. It makes no difference whether a human being jumps from 200 feet or 32,000 feet. After the first few seconds, the human body falls as fast as gravity can make it. So a stuntman falling from a high building and a skydiver falling from an aircraft would hit the ground at approximately the same speed.

A stuntman survives his fall by landing on a huge inflated

airbag with large vents. The impact of the body on the bag blasts air out of the vents, and the result is a massive cushion to slow the fall. The half-pipe works exactly the same way. It consists of a landing pad made of an incredibly strong but gossamer-thin fabric and a compressed-air cylinder, plus a smaller emergency cylinder. When it hits the ground, the half-pipe landing pad inflates instantly, like an airbag in a car, expanding to the size of a swimming pool.

The way to survive the fall is to hit the pad dead center, which is a lot harder to do from 32,000 feet than from 200 feet. From 32,000 feet, even a landing pad the size of a football field would appear as a mere pinprick far below.

To ensure the jumper lands on the pad and nowhere else, each half-pipe is keyed electronically to their free-fall flight suit. Small fins and vanes on the suit move, aiming the suit at the center of the landing pad. If everything works correctly, the person will land in the middle of the pad uninjured. If they miss the pad, or something goes wrong with the equipment, it will be a very hard landing.

[2355 hours]

[Central Australia]

"Mayday! Mayday!" Chisnall yelled desperately into his comm. "Half-pipe malfunction!"

He had instinctively flared his limbs again, slowing his descent to buy himself as much time as possible.

"I'm clear. Use mine!" Price sounded scared, but her words were strictly professional. "Activating emergency strobe and reinflating."

There was a procedure for a half-pipe malfunction, but Chisnall had never heard of anyone using it. At least, not anyone who had survived. There were only seconds left before he was a smear of red on the desert. He twisted around, scanning the ground for the infrared strobe.

There it was!

When Price landed, the air was shunted out of her landing pad, making it useless until it reinflated. The secondary, emergency cylinder could be used to reinflate the pad, but that took time, and time was one thing he didn't have. Landing on a half-deflated pad was only marginally better than landing on solid ground.

Chisnall had already hit the manual override on his wrist, cutting off the signal from his own half-pipe, which was like the song of a siren, luring him to disaster. He angled his arms and legs, aiming for the rapid flicker of the strobe.

The light of the strobe grew, impossibly fast, as he hurtled toward it. He could even see the landing pad now. It looked flat and empty, although the surface was billowing as the air rushed back into it. He tucked his arms and legs to his sides, rolling over onto his back before flaring out again.

"Come left! Come left!" came Angel Six's voice in his comm.

He must have drifted right when he rolled. Chisnall adjusted slightly and was just wondering whether he had overcorrected when a giant hand smacked into his back, followed immediately by another, even harder collision. A crunching sound, followed by blackness.

The Bzadians had first come to Earth in the 1940s, not long after the end of the Second World War. They had hung around for most of the 1950s and quietly disappeared in the mid-1960s, having completed their survey of the planet and, apparently, liking what they saw.

Back in those days, stealth technology was unheard of on Earth, and they were able to fly their stealth rotorcraft without fear of being detected by the primitive radar systems that existed at the time. The only real danger of detection came from the occasional farmer or airline pilot who saw one of the rotorcraft and cried UFO, but those people were generally dismissed as being fruit loops.

Then came the year 2014, when the first transporters began to arrive. Not hovering over Earth's major cities like spaceships out of some sci-fi horror flick, but orbiting once around Earth before beginning a gradual descent through the atmosphere toward the center of Australia.

The transporters had wings like a space shuttle, and like a space shuttle, they were little more than huge gliders, landing on the massive level salt flats of the Australian desert. Each one held nearly 3,000 aliens in stasis tubes, about to be awakened after a fourteen-year journey.

Once down, the transporters were there for good. They

had been built in space and launched in space, for a one-way ticket to Earth. They had no propulsion system capable of breaking free of Earth's gravity. Once they landed, they could never again get off the ground.

The Bzadians said they had come seeking refuge. Their own planet was dying, and they needed just a tiny corner of our world to call their own, to resettle their people. Their own world was a desert planet, and the inaccessible reaches of the Australian deserts suited them perfectly.

Earth governments could hardly refuse. Our first contact with an alien race was an opportunity to demonstrate the goodwill and compassion of the human race. The Australian government, although initially unsure, came under immense pressure from other countries to comply.

In 2015, the aliens lost a transporter when an equipment malfunction caused it to miscalculate its entry and damage its wings. It fell to Earth on the screens of every television channel on Earth. The slow-motion disaster happened over the course of a day, with Bzadians and humans alike helpless to stop it. Three thousand souls extinguished before they even had a chance to wake from stasis. The loss of that craft generated immense public sympathy for the newcomers and helped turn the Australian government's opinion in their favor.

In any case, what choice did the Australians have? The aliens were already there. More transporters began to arrive. And more. Over 6,000 of the massive spaceships dotted the Australian desert before Earth governments began to sense that something was wrong. These first Bzadians were not mere settlers. They were assembling an army.

Alarmed at what they were seeing on satellite imagery, the Australian government hastily threw up a thin ring of defenses around its major cities. On June 17, 2020, "a day of inconceivable treachery," the Bzadian Army attacked Australia's defenses. The Australian Army stood no chance, and within days the cities belonged to the aliens.

The reason for the sudden, shocking attack became clear on July 2 that same year. The skies above Earth turned black as a huge armada approached. Those early transporters were no more than the first drops of a thunderstorm.

Australians were at first allowed, then encouraged, then forced to leave. Their homes and businesses, their schools and shops, were all required for the incoming Bzadian settlers.

Australia became New Bzadia.

Still the other governments of Earth dithered. Appeasement was the policy. Let them have Australia, they said. Nobody wants a war.

And so it was for over three years.

Then came the probing attacks northward to Papua New Guinea, northwest to Indonesia. New Zealand, to the east, was left alone. Too small, too isolated to be bothered with, although Bzadian aircraft made regular sweeps of the country to make sure Earth forces were not using it as a military base.

In Indonesia, one of the first countries to fall, the

conquered population began a vicious guerrilla war against their occupiers. The Bzadian response was quick and brutal. The entire population was eliminated. The aliens were unrestrained by any kind of human morals and saw humans as a subspecies. An animal to be tamed and put to work, or put down if it turned on its master and no longer served a purpose.

The "cleansing" of Indonesia crossed all human boundaries: racial, religious, age, and gender. The alien invaders systematically cleared the country of humans as humans might rid a house of cockroaches. Some managed to escape; those who couldn't, died.

Finally, the world responded. A line was drawn in the sand.

Battle commenced.

Southeast Asia fell quickly, with heavy casualties on the human side, and the invaders headed north. Even the combined weight of the great Asian armies could not hold the alien invaders. The huge landmasses of Asia were lost, along with their vast mineral resources.

Europe was next. The Russian scorched-earth policy slowed them but could not hold them back. The Bzadians had learned from human history and attacked Russia in the summer, the spinning hulls of their huge battle tanks decimating the massed armor of the Russian Army.

They spread west and east, conquering and subduing country after country. The Bzadians were confident that Earth's primitive armies would be no match for their high-tech weapons.

And to some extent they were right. But what they hadn't counted on was the incredible pace of human technological progress. They arrived expecting to fight weapons and machines they had seen in the 1960s. What they came up against were Earth's armies of a new millennium. Stealth fighters, predator drones, and cruise missiles.

Humans had another advantage also. Satellite surveillance. The aliens had not been able to ship to Earth the rockets, nor the tons of rocket fuel required to break a payload free of Earth's atmosphere. Launch facilities in Asia and Europe had been destroyed before they could fall into Bzadian hands. Humans knew what the Bzadians were doing. The Bzadians, for the most part, were blind.

Still, the outcomes of the land battles were never really in doubt. City by city, country by country, Earth fell to the Bzadians.

Finally, the aliens turned their attention to the Americas, the last outpost of humanity.

This presented a whole new problem for them. Geography. The Bzadians were not used to Earth's vast reaches of water. Their own oceans were mainly subterranean, and their knowledge of boatbuilding was confined to rivercraft. They had no knowledge of submarines. A species that had evolved on a planet with little surface water found itself in a war on a planet where two-thirds of the surface was water.

Despite all the invaders' victories, the oceans still belonged to the humans and were guarded by the strength of the combined human navies. The Bzadians' heavy transport aircraft were only good for short distances, and the Pacific and Atlantic Oceans became a moat, defending Fortress America from attack.

Still the Bzadians tried. In 2026, they launched a massive invasion fleet and set course for American shores. A cloud of aircraft buzzed overhead, a protective screen designed to keep the human navies at bay.

It almost worked. The human navies retreated, under attack from a thousand stinging hornets. The invasion fleet surged forward, confident of victory, right into the trap that Earth forces had laid for them. Waiting silently beneath a thermocline, the submarines of forty nations were massed. Operating in concert, they allowed the alien fleet to enter a kill zone before simultaneously unleashing a storm of deadly torpedoes.

It was the first and last time the Bzadians tried a waterborne invasion.

But they did not give up. They attacked overland, crossing the frozen Bering Strait and driving into Alaska in the great Ice War of 2028. It was an ambitious and daring gamble, but the Bzadians were again beaten back as the U.S. forces used the ice itself as one of their most potent weapons. As the summer came and the frozen sea melted, the aliens withdrew, licked their wounds, and consolidated their gains.

The nations that made up North and South America, now collectively known as the Free Territories, watched and waited, preparing for the attacks they knew would come.

And every day the alien transporters kept arriving. The

story about their planet dying was true. The part about needing just a small corner of Earth was not. They wanted it all.

Blackness became a murky world of luminous shapes, fading in and out of Chisnall's vision like vague banks of cloud. He watched, fascinated by the changing shades and rippling patterns, as yet unconcerned by a total feeling of numbness. He felt no fear, no desperation. What would be, would be, and he could do nothing but watch.

The shapes were calling for him now, making terrible primal sounds. And they knew his name.

"Chiiiznaaal!"

"Ryyyaaan!"

One of them moved in for the kill, a dim oval sharpening into eyes, a nose, and fangs that flashed toward his neck.

Except it wasn't aiming for his neck.

The lips sealed on his in a warm, salty kiss that was damp and tasted slightly of peppermint. A flood of hot, moist air flooded his chest. The pressure was too much. He couldn't breathe. Then the lips were gone and the pressure released and the air fled from his lungs.

Again the lips closed on his own, but this time when the pressure released, he found the muscles that controlled his tongue and used them.

"What are you doing?" he asked, realizing that at best it was a blurry mumble. "I'm not dead!"

At that moment, pain hit him everywhere, all at once, a cacophony of agony.

Then the oval shape was back, not covering his face this time but next to it. Soft hands had found their way around his neck and were pulling him—no, just holding him, which sent the pain to a whole new level. But he said nothing and just felt the curves of the body cradling his. The face pulled away and he saw it was Sergeant Brogan, Holly Brogan.

"Are you okay, Lieutenant?" she asked.

He hated the way Brogan said that. "Leff-tenant." There were no *f*'s in *lieutenant.* Why couldn't Australians speak proper English?

"What's your status, Lieutenant?"

He tested his arms, then his legs. They all seemed to work. That meant his back was okay as well. He reached up to his head, and his helmet came away in pieces in his hands. It had done exactly what it was supposed to do. It had absorbed the shock, destroying itself in the process but saving his life.

His back was on fire, as were his legs. In fact, his whole body felt like he had just gone twelve rounds in the ring against Easton Bunker, the battalion boxing champion, and he knew he'd be black and blue the next day. But nothing felt broken. The combat body armor he was wearing beneath his flight suit probably had something to do with that.

"What's your status, Lieutenant?" Brogan repeated.

"Oscar Kilo," Chisnall said weakly. "Oscar Kilo."

He was lying on the floor of the desert. More accurately,

he was lying *in* the floor of the desert. Embedded in it. The first impact he had felt had been the surface of the landing pad. The second had been when he made a small crater in the sand of the desert. As much as the partially inflated half-pipe, it had been the soft sand of Australia herself that had saved him.

The other members of the team were also there, gathered over him.

"Cheese and rice, LT," Monster said. "You one lucky son of a bitch."

"They don't call him Lieutenant Lucky for nothing," Hunter said.

He felt a gentle hand on his forehead. Brogan was leaning over him again, her eyes close to his, looking at his pupils for signs of concussion. Her hands felt their way around his head, pressing gently on his skull. He felt her breath on his cheek. "Are you injured, *Leff-tenant*?" Brogan asked. She was unclipping his body armor, her fingers probing his arms, his legs.

He said nothing and just let her do her work, feeling the pressure, the pain, as her fingertips explored the damaged areas of his body.

Brogan was the perfect soldier: highly trained and cold as ice. But inside her somewhere he knew there was a pretty normal sixteen-year-old girl. Someone with feelings. Some of them for him.

Chisnall shook his head and sat upright, ignoring the shriek of protest from his back. He rolled to one side and stood up on limbs that did not want to hold him. Brogan lent him an arm for support while he steadied himself.

He looked around. It was not as dark in the desert as he expected. Even without his night-vision gear, he could see the shape of mountains to the northeast. The desert floor itself seemed almost luminescent.

A whole night's tabbing lay ahead of them. That was not going to be fun or easy with the state of his back and legs. But nobody had ever said this mission was going to be easy.

Each of them recovered their own gear, hauling in the fabric of the half-pipes in huge armfuls. Chisnall's was still in one piece, although the casing had split open on contact with the desert, spilling the contents all around. The fabric of his landing pad was a large, tightly packed wad. While the others were busy with their gear, he levered open the control hatch with his utility knife, using his flashlight to peer inside.

The trigger in the unit's nose cone should have fired a small explosive to blow the end off the main air cylinder and inflate the pad. The trigger mechanism, although mangled by the crash, looked functional. It was a very simple switch; there was not much that could go wrong with it.

The miniature motherboard was in pieces and there was little point in even looking at that. But if the motherboard was faulty, the system would not have shown as ready. He traced the wires along to the detonator. They looked fine. He slit open the left wire with his knife, exposing the metal core. Nothing wrong there. He slit open the right cable and gritted his teeth slightly.

There it was. Impossible to spot by visual inspection. The metal core of the wire had been removed and replaced with a narrow filament of fuse wire. It would conduct electricity and pass all the circuit tests, but as soon as a high voltage was applied to set off the detonator, it would melt, breaking the circuit. A gap in the wire testified that that was exactly what had happened.

Somebody wanted him dead.

A FACC-E (free-fall air-cushioned container—equipment) had dropped with them. They spread out to search for its signal with their locator packs, with Hunter and Price staying put to dig a big pit in the sand.

"Got it, LT." Monster's normally huge, booming voice was unusually quiet on the comm, reminding Chisnall that they were deep behind enemy lines.

Monster and Wilton brought it in, and they all retrieved the gear they would need for the mission. Night-vision goggles. Bzadian helmets and weapons. Backpacks full of supplies. Everything that had been too dangerous or too heavy to carry with them on the half-pipe drop.

Into the pit went all the half-pipes and cylinders, along with their flight suits and helmets. Brogan tossed in a thermite grenade on a ten-minute timer, and they hurried to fill the pit in, completely burying the gear before they heard the sizzle and felt the heat of the explosion through the sand.

Chisnall slid on his NV goggles and looked around at his team. They stood in a circle, fully kitted up, fully armed.

"God, you're ugly," he said.

Each member of the team had had bone extensions added to their skulls to give their heads the elongated "corn kernel" shape of the aliens. Their skin had been discolored with chemicals that would take years to fade, giving them the mottled green and yellow skin of the alien invaders.

The alien combat helmets they wore were slightly elongated, with a metal rim forming a visor at the front. They also came lower over the ears than most human styles of helmets. The body armor was black and ridged in odd places. Markings on their armor identified them as members of the Bzadian 35th Scout Battalion. Satellite surveillance gave them a good picture of which Bzadian unit was where, and the 35th Scouts had been transferred to Uluru from Perth just the day before.

"Yeah, and you look like something I once left on the sick bay floor at school," Price said, sticking out her forked tongue at him. They had all had the operation, splitting the ends of their tongues in two, like a snake's. Physically at least, they were alien soldiers—"Pukes." So named because their skin looked like the contents of a vomit bag.

"We going kill scumbugz, yezzz," Wilton said in a thick Bzadian accent, effortlessly imitating the strange, buzzing speech of the aliens. "Going kill lotz scumbugz. This our planet now."

Chisnall smiled briefly and pulled a GPS mapping tablet out of his top utility pocket, wincing as the muscles in his back and arm objected to the movement. A flashing orange light indicated their position, and a steady green light showed the location of their target.

"We made good distance," he said. "GPS shows us less than two hundred klicks from our target."

"Dude, that is, like, forever," Wilton muttered.

"Yeah, and if we'd bailed when you first started whining, it would have been four hundred klicks," Brogan said.

Chisnall nodded. Every extra second on the aircraft was almost a kilometer closer to the target.

"Okay, we're Oscar Mike in five. We'll head east until we strike the riverbed," he said. "We'll follow that north, past Mount Morris. Cross the highway and tab overland past Benda Hill up to Uluru. We should do it in four days, if you ladies don't want to stop for a manicure and a back massage."

"Hear that, Wilton?" Price asked. "No more manicures for you."

"Are we there yet?" Hunter grinned.

"You do that all the way, Hunter, and I'm going to hand you over to the Pukes myself," Brogan said.

"Daddy, Mummy's picking on me," Hunter said.

Chisnall ignored him. "Price, did your scope survive the drop okay?"

"Fully functional," Price said.

The scope was a handheld radar system carried by Bzadian soldiers. Theirs had come from a POW.

"Okay, don't take your eyes off it," Chisnall said. "First sign of enemy mobiles, ground or air, and we hit the deck. Cover yourself with your camo sheet and do not move. Is that clear?"

"Not even to scratch arse?" Monster asked.

"They won't see you under your camo, and their thermals won't pick you up either. But they will pick up movement. Once you're down, you don't move a muscle, even if a dingo starts chewing on your leg."

"Rules of engagement, skipper?" Brogan asked.

Chisnall looked at her. "We're in enemy territory," he said. "There are no friendlies here. We might encounter alien civilians; we might encounter children. If it has a gun, then you are cleared to engage. But remember: as far as anyone knows, we are Bzadian soldiers. We don't want to fire unless fired upon."

He tucked away the tablet and stood up, looking around again at the vast nothingness of the Australian desert.

"Okay, weapons check," he said. "Hunter, check the laser comms unit too. We're in trouble if that didn't survive the drop."

They couldn't afford to use radio to communicate with base. The chances of the Bzadians picking up the transmissions were just too great. The laser comms unit fired a precise burst of laser energy at an exact spot in the sky, where a geo-stationary satellite was ready to receive it. It was completely undetectable unless you happened to be in the path of the beam, and since it transmitted for microseconds at a time, that was highly unlikely.

Chisnall checked his own weapons, starting with his coil-gun, a stubby-looking Bzadian rifle that used magnetic fields rather than explosive propellant to fire projectiles. Underneath was a stubby grenade launcher that held two grenades. The rifle clipped onto a spring-loaded bracket across his back. He hit the release button on his right shoulder and the weapon instantly swung up over his shoulder and into his waiting hands. He moved the gun back over his shoulder, ignoring the protests from his back, and felt the automatic holster grab it from him. His sidearm was a needle-gun. It fired long, narrow needles that had incredible range and accuracy.

The others all indicated their weapons were okay.

"Diagnostics on the laser comms all read positive," Hunter said. "We're good to go."

"Good," Chisnall said. "Send the first signal now: 'All down safely, proceeding to the first waypoint.'"

"All down safely, proceeding to the first waypoint." Hunter confirmed the message before keying it in. He unfolded tripodlike legs from the unit and found a relatively flat place to put it. When he activated it, the laser swiveled, automatically orienting itself to a signal from the satellite. There was a brief flash from the top of the unit.

"Message sent and confirmed received," Hunter said. He packed away the comms unit into his backpack.

"Okay, we're Oscar Mike. Tactical column. Hunter, you're

on point," Chisnall said. "Everybody, focus on your sectors. Price's scope won't necessarily pick up foot mobiles. Use your NV and watch for any sign of movement."

Hunter set a brisk pace. Chisnall followed at the rear of the team, struggling on leaden legs. Six Pukes tabbing through the middle of the desert. That was what they looked like. Whether it would be enough to fool any spotters that happened to see them, he wasn't sure.

He didn't dwell on it. There were other things on his mind.

Someone wanted him dead.

He had spent an hour in Angel Chariot's bomb bay before the mission, personally checking all the half-pipes, including the wires. They had all been fine. After that, the plane had been under heavy guard. Chisnall had been told to expect trouble on this mission. It wasn't specified, but it was clear that no one was to be trusted. No one.

But the traitor had made their way into a top-secret, heavily guarded hangar, levered open the control unit, replaced the wire, and closed the unit, right under the noses of the guards. It would have taken a ghost to do that.

The sheer audacity of it was unbelievable.

Only six people apart from him had access to that hangar. One of them, the pilot of Angel Chariot, had died over the Australian desert.

The other five were all here with him.

3. OSCAR MIKE

[MISSION DAY 2]
[0120 hours]
[Central Australia]

CHISNALL STARTED THE NEXT DAY WITH A LIST OF FIVE suspects, but by the end of the day he was able to narrow it down to four.

It was a simple process of elimination.

His team was the best of the best. They had been selected from the top recruits at the 4th Reconnaissance Team base at Fort Carson, Colorado.

Even to get chosen to go to Fort Carson was an honor, although none of them had known it at the time. The initial selection process was a simple one: paintball. With the military's backing, paintball had grown from a minor pursuit to the largest sport in the Americas. Those who showed consistent ability, intelligence, and stamina were selected for an initial screening, using ICP modeling and genetic testing to determine their final height. If they were likely to grow tall, they were not selected. If, after all the screening, they grew too tall anyway, they were dropped from the program.

After the first year, recruits who showed leadership qualities were put through an officer's program. They still had to undergo all the physical and military training of the other recruits, but on top of that, they had hours of study in leadership, strategies, and tactics.

Chisnall had topped the officer program. It had been a surprise to everyone, most of all him. All the smart money had been on Bryan Brown, a loud, tough, and competent football player from Iowa. Chisnall was nothing like Bryan. He was not even particularly noticeable, with a slight (but wiry) build, sandy hair, and nondescript features. He did not look special. But according to his personnel file, he quietly, and with a minimum of fuss, got on with the job, bringing an extraordinary intelligence and an ability to solve problems to the tasks at hand. Right now, he would have laughed to see that note in his file; his intelligence and problem-solving ability seemed to have completely deserted him. One of his team was a traitor, and he had no idea who.

Chisnall had been warned about the cold nights, but nothing had prepared him for the icy wind that cut in from the east, blasting his nose and cheeks. It was strange how the desert could be scorching hot by day and freezing cold at night. He almost considered pulling down his combat visor to block it out, but none of the others had done so, and he didn't want to look soft in front of them. Nobody wanted to be the first to seem weak.

After about an hour's hard tabbing, they found themselves in a strange world. A field of rocks, huge sandstone formations embedded in the sand. A place completely devoid of any form of plant life. It was as if the rocks had sprouted up through the desert.

In the green world of Chisnall's NV goggles, the odd shapes began to look familiar. One was a hand with thumb raised like a hitchhiker. Another was a dog, up on its hind legs and begging. He walked past a smaller rock, no taller than him, a slightly lopsided Egyptian-style pyramid, and another, much larger, that was clearly a huge tongue pointed upward—the desert pulling faces at the night sky. The cold wind whistled around and through the rock sculptures, making eerie moaning and whistling sounds. Alien sounds.

It was an alien landscape in a country overrun by aliens. Yet the rocks were no more alien than he was. They must have been there for millions of years, changing only gradually in that slow Earth way of doing things, where a 100,000 years was just a blink of an eye.

Chisnall glanced up as he walked, scanning the sky as if he could see the satellites that were watching him, watching every move and every decision he made. For a moment, he felt he was on show. An actor on a stage. If he made a bad decision and compromised the mission, there would be no hiding it from the observers back at ACOG. But there was more at stake here than his embarrassment. Their lives were at stake—and depending on what they found inside Uluru, the fate of the Free Territories could be at stake too.

Three hours later, the satellites were made useless.

The sandstorm arrived not as a solid wall, the way sandstorms appeared in movies, but as gentle fingers of sand that tugged at their ankles in the dark. Within half an hour, the swirling coils of dust were up to their knees, and less than an hour after it started, they were pulling down their visors against the blustery, grainy winds.

"Everybody down," Chisnall said as the force of the sandstorm crept up from mild buffeting to hard thrashing. "Interlock camo sheets."

Every member of the team carried a camouflage sheet for concealment. As the winds whipped up further and further, a thousand knives of dust and sand slashing against their body armor, they interlocked the sheets and crawled underneath, using their body weight to hold down the edges against the desert fury above.

Their low profile gave them good protection from the storm, but even so, it was as though claws were tearing at the fabric. Sand trickled inside through any tiny opening, a gap under the edge of the sheets, a missed Velcro joint, a pinhole spy-hole. Brogan had turned on her flashlight and they could see the wild undulations of the sheets under the power of the storm above.

Chisnall checked the time. Every minute spent under the shelter, waiting for the storm to subside, was a further delay in reaching their destination. And these storms could go on for days. The only upside was the perfect concealment it gave them from enemy eyes. No alien patrols would be wandering around in this, and their aircraft could only fly above it, unable to peer down through the hurricane of sand.

A ripping sound filled the space under the blanket, followed by the pungent smell of putrefied eggs. There was a chorus of groans from the team.

"Monster, that's awful," Wilton said.

"That's a weapon of mass destruction," Hunter said.

"Nothing ever changes, bro," Price said amid the laughter.

"The Monster's bottom is barking today," Monster said.

"Howling like a wolf, if you ask me," Chisnall said.

"I think I'd rather take my chances with the sandstorm," Wilton said.

"You'd better pray it doesn't last much longer," Brogan said. "We could be stuck here for days."

"With Monster farting," Hunter said. "God help us."

"That's what you need to pray for," Chisnall said. "God to help us."

"No use me praying," Monster said. "The Monster is big sinner. If God hears Monster pray, he'll say, 'Whatever Monster prays for, I'll do opposite.'"

"How about you, Price?" Chisnall asked. "You want to pray for us?"

"Wouldn't know where to start, bro," Price said. "Let Wilton do it. He's all religious."

"The hell I am," Wilton said.

"Then why do you keep that Bible and that cross and everything in your bunk back in Fort Carson?" Price asked.

"My family sent them to me," Wilton said. "Seems wrong to chuck stuff like that."

"But you ain't religious?" Hunter asked.

"Nope. My family is," Wilton said. "All of them. Parents, sisters, uncles, cousins, the whole damn tribe. I always wanted to be. When I was young, I used to pray to God every night and ask him to make me a Christian. But he never did."

"Angel Five, you are one weird dude," Price said.

[0430 hours]

[Officers' Quarters, Republican Guard HQ, Uluru Military Base]

Lieutenant Yozi Gonzale woke, feeling the subtle shift in the air pressure in the room as the sandstorm howled outside. Sandstorms always woke him. On Bzadia, such storms were more frequent, almost an everyday event, but they were also shorter and much milder—a soft cloud of blanketing dust, compared to the vicious whorls of abrasive sand that scoured the deserts of New Bzadia.

He lay awake and listened to the storm. Many of his comrades had no trouble getting used to the long Earth days and even longer nights. Half as long again as the days and nights on Bzadia. For some reason, Yozi had never managed to adjust. Fortunately, he had never needed much sleep, and apart from the boredom, the long Earth nights did not worry him, even in winter when the nights went on forever here in New Bzadia. *Australia,* the humans had called it, when they had owned the country.

"Os-trail-yuh." He sounded out the word. No matter how hard he tried, the sibilant *S* sound of the humans came out as a Bzadian buzz. "Ozz-trail-yuh."

His promotion to the Republican Guards had been hard earned. Months on the front lines. One vicious battle after another. Many of his soldiers were lost as the humans dug their toes in and refused to give up ground.

Yozi listened to the discordant music of the sandstorm outside and was glad that he was inside the secure stone walls of the officers' quarters. Hopefully the storm will have subsided before he was due to go on patrol at first light.

After a while, the others hunkered down and tried to get some shut-eye. Chisnall just listened to the raging sand winds above and thought through the plans for the mission. Was it possible that someone on his team was a traitor to the human race?

He ran through the list of suspects in his mind. It was a pretty small list.

Hunter. English. If there was ever a soldier you'd want to have at your side in a difficult situation, it was Stephen Huntington. Never afraid of a fight, no matter what the consequences, and he'd usually be the last man standing.

Hunter had been hardened like steel, forged in the fires that were the British refugee camps in Massachusetts and Maine. With the fall of Great Britain, he and his working-class family were abruptly thrust into a tent ghetto. Somehow they survived the harsh Maine winters and a society ruled by the fist and the broken bottle.

Amid the grime of the unpaved streets, Hunter had cracked knuckles until he was the one everyone—even the adults—feared. Hunter had confessed to Chisnall that he would have killed or been killed if he hadn't been hauled off by the "coppers" and sent to a juvenile hall.

It was there that his prowess at paintball was noticed.

The army had given Hunter discipline. Had shaped his steel into a deadly sword.

Holly Brogan was Chisnall's sergeant and the only trained medic on the team. Tough, capable, deadly, and gorgeous. She looked like a cheerleader but was the battalion's unarmed combat champion. Look like a butterfly, sting like a bee, Chisnall had thought when he first saw her fight.

Brogan was Australian. Her country was overrun, her parents killed. If anybody had a reason to hate the aliens, she did. But she didn't let emotion control her actions. Not at all. She was clinical in everything she did. She was a by-the-book soldier, but the "book" that she followed existed for a reason. Many men and women had died so that the military could develop methods and rules for combat. She had never been selected for officer school, which surprised Chisnall, but she had quickly earned promotion to sergeant and was invaluable in that role. This mission was a chance for her to strike back at those who had killed her parents.

Trianne Price was a ghost. The Kiwi Phantom. She could move through the night like a soft breath of wind, and even if you were looking for her, you would be lucky to notice that she was there. You never saw her coming; you never knew she'd been. That ability had got her selected for this, the first ever Angel Team recon operation. Chisnall knew little about her except that she had had a tough childhood. There were scars on the light coffee-colored skin of her arms, some of which looked like cigarette burns. She seldom talked about her upbringing, but, like Hunter, she had been forged in the fires of her youth. Her way of avoiding pain was to simply avoid being seen. To not be noticed. She was very good at it.

But it was strange how the Bzadians had left New Zealand alone. A small country, sure, but right on their doorstep. It would have been like taking candy from a baby. Yet they hadn't. Could the New Zealand government have entered in some kind of secret pact with the aliens? It seemed unlikely.

Blake Wilton was Canadian. A champion snowboarder with an unusually wide face and small eyes. Wilton had been selected for one reason only. He was the best shot in the battalion, and that included the adult soldiers in the other recon teams. A specialist sharpshooter, but kind of a weird guy. He operated on a different wavelength than the rest of the team. Chisnall often thought Wilton felt he had to prove himself as tough as the others in order to be accepted. But it really wasn't that that set him apart—he was just a little different. Chisnall had had to weigh up the odds carefully before including him on the team, but in the end it came down to his shooting. A rifle in Wilton's hands was worth ten in anyone else's.

That left Specialist Panyoczki, Janos, known as Monster. The crazy, squat, barrel-chested Hungarian. His family's escape from war-torn Hungary was the stuff of nightmares, and perhaps because of that he took life by the neck and squeezed every drop out of it. His jovial exterior did not quite hide a fearless, resourceful individual. And his sheer physical power made him invaluable in those kinds of situations where brute force was the only answer. Surely a spy or a traitor would try to be as unobtrusive as possible, and unobtrusive Monster definitely was not. Or was that the perfect cover?

When Hunter had first arrived at Fort Carson, he had been ready to take on anyone who got in his way. He was on the verge of getting kicked out of camp, and Chisnall, recognizing some kind of potential in him, had tried to reason with him. Hunter had knocked Chisnall down. If not for Monster, Chisnall would have been in for a severe beating. But Monster had intervened and even Hunter was no match for the Hungarian. Somehow, after that, the three of them had become friends.

Chisnall would have trusted any of the team with his life.

He had trusted them all with his life. But one of them had betrayed that trust.

Chisnall's mind kept coming back to the hangar. If anybody could have slipped in and out of there without being noticed, it was Price.

He had no evidence, though. And his gut instinct hardly even counted as a clue.

The storm was a small one, just a baby compared to the huge sandstorms that could rage through the heart of Australia. Less than an hour after they had hunkered down under the protection of the camo sheets, they were on the move again.

"What is at Uluru, anyway?" Monster asked, taking a sip of water from his throat tube.

"A ruddy great rock," Hunter replied.

Monster laughed heartily. "Yes, my dude. The Monster knows this. You know this. The generals also they know this. So what are we looking for?"

"Your brain," Price said. "It's been missing since 2015."

"Keep your eyes on your sector," Chisnall said.

"This mission is very dangerous," Monster insisted. "Angel Team has right to know what's at Uluru."

Chisnall stared at Monster but could read nothing from the back of his head. Was this just an innocent question?

"If I knew what was going on at Uluru," Chisnall said, "I would just tell HQ and we could all go home and sleep in nice warm beds. You think I like traipsing through the desert, living on a diet of alien pond scum?"

"Is that what's in those tubes?" Brogan asked. "I just thought some butt wipe in supply got his cartons mixed up and gave us a consignment of hemorrhoid cream."

"So nobody knows what's at Uluru?" Monster was not giving up.

Chisnall said, "Whatever's there, it's giving the top brass the screaming meemies. They badly want to know what is going on inside that rock."

"I doubt that, LT," Brogan said. "If they really cared about this mission, they would have sent along some real soldiers instead of this bunch of no-hoper, bottom-feeding trailer trash."

"You including yourself in that assessment, soldier?" Chisnall asked.

"Sir, yes, sir!" Brogan snapped out.

"It's a pie factory," Price said. "I got it from Bonnie Kelaart in transport. She heard a couple of generals discussing it. The Pukes are building this massive pie factory, and after they've conquered the rest of the world, they're going to keep us all in farms and turn us into juicy meat pies."

"The Monster won't eat pie with you in it, Grandma," Monster said.

"Pukes are not gonna conquer the world, dude," Wilton said. "We're gonna kick their asses back to Mars."

"They aren't from Mars, you plonker," Hunter said.

"Price, there's just one problem with your theory," Chisnall said.

"Yes, sir?"

"The Pukes are all vegetarians."

"Not true, sir," Price said.

"Then why are we eating green slime and not roasting a koala over a fire for dinner?" asked Chisnall.

"That's just what they want us to think," Price said. "Until the pie factory is ready."

"Koala pie sounds good," Monster said.

"There's no reason for the mission," Wilton contributed. "It's just a test of our disguises. The brass wants to find out if we can really fool the Pukes. We're guinea pigs."

"Don't believe everything you think," Brogan said.

"Just stay focused on your sector," Chisnall said, shaking his head.

"So what's your plan to get us in, skipper?" Hunter asked. "Just going to rock on up to the front door and knock?"

"Specialist Huntington, that part of the plan is way above your security level," Chisnall replied. Now Hunter was asking "innocent" questions.

"Why's that, then?" Hunter asked.

"I can't answer that," Chisnall said.

"Why not?"

"That's also above your security level."

"Why wouldn't they just let us in?" Wilton asked. "We look like Pukes. We sound like Pukes."

"You smell like puke," Price added.

"As far as they know, we are Pukes," Wilton said. "Why can't we just waltz on in?"

"If they DNA test us, we be behind bars in two seconds," Monster said.

"If they DNA tested you, you'd be in a zoo," Hunter said.

"They won't," Chisnall said. "There are hundreds of thousands of Pukes wandering around this part of the desert. It's their biggest military base. They don't have time to DNA test everyone. And besides, why would they?"

"I heard that, genetically, we're only one percent different from the Pukes," Wilton said.

"Yeah, well, genetically, we're only one percent different from chimpanzees, but you don't see me climbing trees and eating bananas with my feet," Hunter said.

"Yeah," Wilton said, "but don't it make you wonder how a species that evolved on another planet, hundreds of light-years away, could share our DNA?"

"Wilton, a lot of scientists with brains a lot bigger than yours are trying to work that out as we speak," Chisnall said. "What those scientists are *not* doing is tabbing through the Australian desert, watching your sector."

"Are we there yet?" Hunter asked.

The first enemy aircraft appeared above Mount Morris just as light was beginning to color the eastern sky.

"Air mobile on the scope," Price said, long before they could see or hear the craft. "Slow mover."

"Cover, cover, cover," Chisnall said. "Radio silence until Phantom gives us the all clear."

He flipped his own camo sheet off the top of his backpack and spread it out quickly on the ground. It immediately picked up the colors and patterns of what was underneath it, and he locked them in before sliding underneath.

They had been walking on rock that was reddish in some places, a mix of gray and yellow in others. From above, even from a few feet away, he would appear only as a mound of rock.

There was a viewing hole near each corner of the blanket, just a pinhole. He put his eye to the closest one and waited. He could hear the craft now. It was going to pass close overhead. There was just enough light in the sky for him to see it.

It was a rotorcraft, the Puke equivalent of a helicopter, although the blades were below and internal, giving the appearance of a large saucer in the sky.

The sudden appearance of the craft worried him. Were they searching for his team? Did they know about the mission? A rotorcraft in this part of the desert had to be looking for something.

It moved off slowly to the southwest. Price's voice came over the comm a few minutes later with the all clear. Chisnall sat up and folded his camo sheet. Around him, five rocky lumps morphed into soldiers.

"One more klick and we'll be near the river," Chisnall said. "We should make that easily before it gets too light. There's a small depression in the rock below a cliff face. We'll camp there during the daylight hours. It'll give us some shadow, and a bit of cover."

At the dry riverbed, they treated themselves to a meal of the alien food-in-a-tube and a self-heating drink sachet that tasted like blood.

Chisnall checked his GPS. They had covered over thirty kilometers. Good going for the first night. His legs and back were aching and he dry-swallowed a painkiller.

"Wilton, take the first watch," he said. "Then Price, Hunter, Brogan. Monster, you take the last."

Nods and grunts acknowledged the instruction. Chisnall looked around the faces of the team, spending longer on Price than the others. Did he trust her to take watch? Did he trust any of them? Not after what had happened. But there was no choice. Watch had to be kept, and if he left out any of the team, that would just make his suspicions plain.

The sun was stretching its arms on the eastern horizon, and with the day came the bush flies. Clouds of them, unbothered by waving hands or insect repellent. They went for the eyes, nose, and mouth—anything moist.

Chisnall watched Monster squeeze a hefty amount of green goo into his mouth from the tube. Flies covered his lips and would occasionally dart inside when he opened his mouth. It didn't seem to worry Monster. He just kept on chewing, only stopping to grin at Chisnall with teeth covered in green with tiny black flecks.

Chisnall gave up trying to eat in the open air and retreated under his camo sheet. Squashing the flies that came under with him, he ate his meal in the cool darkness beneath. He had chosen his position carefully—against the cliff face, in a small V-shaped ridge slightly away from the others.

The rock was hard, but they each had a self-inflating sleeping bag. After eating, Chisnall lay facedown on top of his. He tried lying on his back, but a wash of fiery pain quickly changed his mind. Facedown was a little more comfortable and he could easily have slept, but didn't. He didn't even bother taking off his body armor. He lay down as if sleeping but kept his eye to one of the pinholes. If anyone approached with murder on their mind, he would be ready.

The day began. The heat rose. Even under the thermal camo sheet, it became uncomfortably hot. Chisnall sipped water to keep hydrated and tried to stretch the pain out of his back and legs. He kept one hand on his sidearm, just in case.

He scanned the riverbed in both directions. To the northeast was the squatting bulk of Mount Morris. Anywhere else in the world, it would have been called a hill rather than a mountain, but in this flat world, it towered over its surroundings.

When Chisnall was eleven, he had gone to summer camp. They had hiked high into the mountains, to a clearing with log cabins. The camp helpers were mostly older teens. There had been tree climbing, mudslides, and ziplines, but the best thing about it was the feeling of being away from adult supervision most of the time.

It felt like an exciting adventure.

At the beginning, this mission had had the same kind of feeling. The six of them, out on their own. No adults to tell them what to do. But the tampering with his half-pipe had changed all that. This was no longer an adventure. It was no longer fun. It had turned deadly serious. He would have given anything to be back at that camp.

4. HUNTER

THROUGH THE PINHOLE IN HIS CAMO SHEET, CHISNALL saw that Price had pulled a prizzem (a kind of miniature Bzadian football) out of her pack and was tossing it up in the air. She tossed it to Wilton, who caught it deftly and flicked it on to Brogan. Hunter moved closer, sat beside them, and joined in the game.

The four of them tossed the ball back and forth aimlessly for a few minutes. They looked tired, but it was hard to go to sleep when the day was just beginning.

"What's the LT like, Brogan?" Price asked in a quiet voice. "You know him better than any of us."

She clearly didn't think her voice would carry that far, or she thought Chisnall was already asleep. But he had unusually good hearing and was wide-awake.

"What do you mean by that?" Brogan asked.

Price shrugged. "Didn't mean anything. Just asking a question."

Brogan glanced over toward Chisnall before replying. "He's a good sort. He's all right."

"How'd he get the medal?" Wilton asked, stretching to catch a high ball from Price.

Under the camo sheet, Chisnall's hand instinctively reached toward his left breast pocket. The medal was not there, of course. It was in his locker back at base. The medal earned him a lot of respect among the other soldiers, but its presence reminded him of something he'd rather forget. Two years before, during the Ice Wars, he had been attached as an observer to a forward command post. When the Bzadians made a big push, he had found himself behind enemy lines. What had happened next had earned him the Distinguished Service Medal and nightmares that didn't seem to fade with time.

"I don't know," Brogan said. She was lying, but only Chisnall knew that.

"You should be honored to be serving under a genuine war hero," Hunter said.

"He doesn't look like a hero," Wilton said.

"What does a hero look like, Wilton?" Hunter asked.

"Not like the LT, that's for sure," said Wilton.

"That's what makes him so dangerous," Brogan said. "If he was ten feet tall and bulletproof, everyone would treat him that way. But he just looks ordinary."

"Harmless," Price agreed.

"By the time you figure out that he's really the meanest, deadliest son of a butcher in the valley, it's already too late," Brogan said.

"Are we talking about the same dude?" Wilton asked. "Our LT? The fearless leader who's so tough that he's already gone for a cup of tea and a lie-down."

"Think what you like," Brogan said. "I'd tell you not to underestimate him, but that's pointless. The moment you look at him, you've already underestimated him."

Chisnall grinned. Not entirely true, but it didn't hurt your reputation with the troops to have your sergeant shovel around a little awe and mystique.

"As for the lie-down," Brogan said, "have you forgotten that the LT landed on a deflated half-pipe? Must have knocked the pudding out of his body. I'm surprised he can even walk. But how many times have you heard him complain?"

"I guess," Wilton said.

Brogan tossed the ball to Hunter and stood up, walking toward Chisnall's position.

He watched her approach. She had already removed her body armor in preparation for sleeping, and the tight Bzadian battle tunic and leggings were damp from the night's sweat and the beginning of the day's heat. They clung to her body like a swimsuit.

She stood over him and he heard her voice through the fabric of the camo sheet.

"Awake, LT?"

"Am now."

"How's the legs?"

He peeled back a corner of the sheet and twisted his head to look up at her.

"All good."

"Really." It was clear she didn't believe him. "Thought I saw you lagging a bit on the last section."

"I wasn't lagging. I was just enjoying the scenery."

"I'd better have a look, eh?"

"At the scenery?"

"At your legs."

"Got nothing better to do?"

"Nope."

She went to her backpack and returned with her own camo sheet. Interlocking one edge of her sheet with his, she wedged a couple of sticks into a crack in the rock to create a bivouac. Her flashlight flicked on and the silver thermal underside of the makeshift tent lit up like a carnival.

To be safe, Chisnall turned his comm mike off, and she did the same.

"I'm so glad you're still alive," she said in a low voice, and kissed him gently on the cheek.

"Not in front of the children," he said quietly.

"God, Ryan, I was so worried," she said, lying down next to him.

"Holly, don't," he said.

"What's the matter?" she asked.

"You shouldn't even be on this mission," he said. "I specifically requested that you not be included."

"And I specifically requested to be on the team," she said. "Why didn't you want me along? Got your eye on Price?"

"You know that's not true," he said. "I'm just not sure I could take it if you got killed or injured."

"*You* almost were," she said. "How do you think I felt?"

"That's what I'm talking about. That's why you shouldn't be here," he said.

"I'm the best one for the job, and you know it," she said.

He was silent for a moment. She *was* the best one for the job. The best soldier he had ever met and a trained medic, and she spoke the Bzadian dialects like a native. If not for their relationship, she would have been the first one he would have picked for the mission.

He said, "That isn't going to make it any easier if one of us gets killed."

"Better than sitting back at camp worrying."

Chisnall was silent. She had a point.

They had been going out for six months, but they had kept it secret because of the camp's strict rules outlawing relationships between soldiers. It was a romance of sneaky meetings and stolen moments. He wondered sometimes if she would have looked at him twice if they had met in another place, under different circumstances.

"I'd better have a look at your legs. Where does it hurt most?" she asked.

"Everywhere," he said.

"Let's have a look, then, shall we?" she said.

"Yes, doctor."

She unclipped the body armor from his legs, then gently peeled back the cuff of his leggings.

"Hmmm," she said.

"What's the prognosis, doctor?"

"Take 'em off," she said.

"My legs? They're not detachable."

"Your leggings—unless you want me to do it for you."

"I'll manage," Chisnall said. He unfastened his Bzadian army leggings and Brogan helped him ease them off.

"Hmmm," she said again.

He twisted around to look. In the glow of Brogan's flashlight, he could see that the skin down the backs of his legs was dark and purplish, with vivid patches of red. On top of the green-yellow mottling of the Bzadian skin coloring, it created a truly nauseating mixture of colors. He twisted back.

"How does that feel?" she asked, gently touching his calf.

"Was that you, or did I just get stung by a bee?" he asked.

"Grit your teeth," she said, which didn't sound promising. He gritted.

She pressed firmly on the back of his thigh with what felt like a sharp knife, heated white-hot—but when he looked, it was only her fingers.

"Hematoma," she said. "I'd better have a look at your back."

She helped him again with the body armor and removed the battle tunic for him when he had trouble twisting his shoulders around to do it. From her drawing in of breath, it was clear his back was worse than his legs.

"Will I live?" he asked.

"If we could preserve this, it could be an exhibit in a museum of modern art," she said. "Very psychedelic. Any doctor would confine you to a week in the hospital."

"Just as well you're not a doctor," Chisnall said.

"You're in no shape to continue this mission," she said.

He was quiet for a moment, knowing she was probably right. "I wish I had that choice," he said eventually.

"You've taken some painkillers?"

"Yep."

"Working?"

"Nope."

"I'll put some topical analgesic on it for you," Brogan said. "At least you might be able to sleep."

"Thanks," Chisnall said.

She disappeared to get it out of her backpack and was back a moment later, pulling on rubber gloves. Then she squeezed the ointment onto her hands, warming it for a moment.

"You're sure this stuff works on humans?" Chisnall asked. All their equipment and supplies were Bzadian army issue.

"That's what they tell us," Brogan said. She spread it softly on his skin, starting with his calves and working her way up. The mere touch of her hands was like fire but she kneaded his flesh gently, massaging in the cream. Slowly, the pain in his legs softened to a dull ache.

"What are you two doing in there?" Price called.

"Playing doctor," Brogan said.

"Why do officers get all the fun?" Hunter said.

"Yeah, this is real fun," Chisnall said. It felt as though Brogan were sandpapering the skin off his shoulders and rubbing salt in the raw, bloodied flesh beneath. He held his breath to stop from crying out, until the painkiller took effect and his shoulders returned to something near normal.

She finished, stripped off the gloves, and lay down on her back next to him. For a moment they really were just two teenagers on a camping trip, not two soldiers behind enemy lines on a vital and deadly mission. He felt like kissing her.

"Ryan, what's really going on? Something tells me there's more to this mission than meets the eye."

The fabric of the bivouac moved a little. Perhaps it was just a brief puff of breeze, but something told him otherwise. Brogan opened her mouth to continue, but Chisnall held a finger to his lips. He cocked his head, listening. There! Was that just the slightest shuffle of a footstep outside?

He nodded to Brogan, who caught his meaning instantly. She reached down, gripped the edge of the camo sheet, and flung it back.

Hunter was squatting just outside. He looked awkward and embarrassed.

"Shouldn't you be on watch?" Brogan asked.

"Just wanting a word with the skipper," Hunter said.

"Go ahead," Chisnall said.

"It can wait," Hunter said. "It was just . . . Nah, I'll talk to you later."

He walked away, down to the riverbed. Chisnall watched him go. How long had he been standing there, listening to their conversation? Did he really have something to say, or was that just an excuse?

Brogan closed the flap again. "We're in-country now," she said. "About time you filled me in."

"Can't do that, soldier," Chisnall said.

"What's the reason for all the secrecy?" Brogan asked.

"I have very specific orders," Chisnall replied.

"Back at Fort Carson, you weren't a strict follower of orders," Brogan said, and the side of her leg brushed against his. He moved his leg away. This was not the time, nor the place.

"We're not back at Fort Carson," Chisnall said.

"Who picked the team?" Brogan asked.

"I had some say in it."

"What jerk picked Wilton?" she asked. "Every time he opens his mouth, you just don't know what's going to come out of it. I'm terrified that he's going to give the game away to the Pukes once we get inside the base."

"This jerk picked him," Chisnall said. "Wilton's a little loose. But who else do you know who could shoot the eye out of a fast-moving eagle at five hundred meters, and do it three times in a row?"

"He's got that," Brogan admitted. "But it's not going to be much help if we're sitting in a Puke jail cell or blindfolded and lined up against a wall."

"Let's hope it doesn't come to that."

"Now Price I understand. If we'd left it up to the Kiwi Phantom, she'd have been inside that rock and back out by now and the Pukes would never know she'd been there. But what about Monster? He's not exactly the quiet, stealthy type."

Chisnall laughed. "True. But if it really hits the fan, is there anyone else you'd rather have on your side?"

"Another slow mover heading our way," Hunter's voice said in his ear.

Chisnall flicked his mike on. "Copy that. All Angels remain in cover."

He flicked the mike off again and moved his eye back to one of the pinholes. The menacing, rounded shape of an enemy rotorcraft appeared low over the riverbed.

It was quartering the desert. This was not just a regular patrol.

"They're searching for something," he said.

"For us?" Brogan asked. "Why would they be searching for us?"

"I don't know. I don't see how they'd know about us. Maybe they're just being careful."

He watched the saucerlike shape for a few moments until it moved off to the south.

"How does it feel to be back?" he asked.

"In Australia" was the unfinished end of the sentence.

Brogan shook her head. "It was ten years ago. I was just a kid. And I grew up in Sydney. The outback is just as foreign to me as it is to you."

"I know," Chisnall said. "But it's still your country. Don't you feel some sense of belonging? Of ownership?"

"A little," she said. "More a feeling of injustice."

"It must have been hard to leave," Chisnall said.

"You could say that," Brogan said. "That was the night my parents were killed."

"I didn't know that. I'm sorry," Chisnall said.

"That last night . . ." Brogan paused.

Chisnall said nothing, giving her some space.

"We were trying to get out," Brogan said. "Part of the Darwin evacuation. My dad was government, so we were on the Pukes' restricted list. But we had false identities, disguises, the whole works. We were actually on the ship and it was heading out to sea when the Bzadians found out. They . . ."

"It's okay," Chisnall said. "You don't have to talk about it."

"They sank the ship. The whole bloody ship."

"Oh my God. You were on the *Campbelltown*! You never told me that."

The sinking of the *Campbelltown,* a passenger liner full of civilians, was one of the worst atrocities of the evacuation of Australia.

"They sank it because my parents were on it. Only a handful of us survived."

He looked at her. Tears were freely flowing down her cheeks, although she made no sound. Chisnall put out a hesitant hand and touched her on the shoulder. She moved closer and he put his arm around her shoulders, holding her.

His tortured back screamed fire, despite the painkillers, but still he drew her close.

After a few moments, she let out one tense, constricted sob and then was silent.

"You'd better get some sleep," he said.

"We all had," Brogan said, making no attempt to move.

"Better find your own spot," Chisnall said after a moment. "We don't want to give the others the wrong idea."

"That could be a little awkward," Brogan agreed. She sat up.

He found himself wishing she would stay. But the focus had to be the mission. He couldn't afford any distractions. Brogan dismantled the bivouac and spread his camo sheet back out over him. He watched her as she strode back toward the river.

I can't afford any distractions.

He held that thought for a while. Then, as the sun rose higher and the day heated up, and despite his best intentions, he slept.

Later, the wind came again, bringing the desert with it. This time the sandstorm was longer but not as ferocious. Chisnall hunkered down under his camo sheet and knew that the others would be doing the same. The storm lessened, then gradually dissipated, growling up in sporadic bursts until it finally died away altogether. He didn't mind the daytime sandstorms. They gave them good cover from the Bzadians and blocked some of the heat of the sun.

It didn't occur to him till later that they also blocked the view of the satellites that were monitoring them, nor that that might suit the purposes of one particular member of the team.

Night falls slowly in the desert. As the sun sank below the horizon, it was as if a painter had taken an airbrush to the western sky, creating a work of art in rich orange and red hues, streaked with violet.

A small yellowish brown lizard, its body covered with a netlike pattern, camped on a rock just in front of Chisnall's nose, completely oblivious to the soldier under the camo sheet just a few inches away.

Chisnall stirred, and the lizard, startled at the rock coming to life, darted under a clump of porcupine grass.

Chisnall awoke with a strange feeling.

Something is wrong.

He felt cold, but not physically. The shivering was much deeper than that. He'd asked his mother about the feeling once when he was younger, and she'd said it came from his soul. He wasn't so sure about that, but he did know that each time the strangeness came, it always meant bad things. Like the night the army men, in their bright, shiny dress uniforms and white gloves, had knocked on the door in the middle of the night to give them the news about his father. Chisnall sat up. His muscles seemed to have turned into cold chewing gum while he slept, and he tried to twist and stretch to get some movement back into them. He crawled out from under his camo sheet and painfully stood up, scanning around them for any sign of danger.

Monster was on watch.

"Anything on the scope?" Chisnall asked.

Monster shook his head. "Plenty of air mobiles up north, but here is quiet. Thought I picked up some foot mobiles one hour ago, but is turn out to be kangaroos."

They were clear. Yet the shivering of his soul was not diminishing. He shrugged it off. They were in the heart of New Bzadia. Everything around them, everybody, was a danger. Perhaps it was just nerves.

"Get 'em up," Chisnall said.

Monster grinned and called out, "Okay, my dudes, up, up, up. Is beautiful evening in Camp Chisnall, and we have lots fun activities for you."

There was a chorus of groans.

"What's for breakfast?" Wilton asked, emerging from under his sheet.

"Green toothpaste," Chisnall replied cheerfully. "Smells like vomit, tastes like phlegm, and gives you the most colorful poop."

"Do Pukes really eat this stuff?" Wilton grumbled.

"It's their army rations," Brogan said. "They probably hate it as much as we hate our MREs."

Meals ready to eat had been the bane of the combat soldier's life since forever.

"I'd give my right arm for an MRE right about now," Wilton said.

"Just eat your greens or you can't have pudding," Brogan said.

Chisnall laughed and looked around. "Somebody go wake Hunter. Tell him he can't sleep all day and all night too."

"LT!" There was something in Price's voice.

Chisnall's primary weapon was in his hands before he even had time to think. He was on his feet, scanning the horizon.

"Over here," Price said, her voice coming in gulps between short breaths. She had peeled back a corner of Hunter's camo sheet.

Specialist Stephen Huntington was dead.

His face was contorted and red, as if he had been fighting for breath. There was froth around his mouth and a dribble of vomit down his cheek. His eyes were fixed, wide and staring.

"Drop the camo," Chisnall said. "Move back slowly." He was conscious of the others crowding around. "Get back, all of you."

"What the—" Wilton started.

"Brogan, if he can't be quiet, shut him up for me," Chisnall said.

He extended the long snout of his weapon and lifted the sheet, flicking it up and away down the rock. Hunter was still in his sleeping bag, but his body was not relaxed. It was distorted in hideous contortions, his arms and legs locked at strange angles beneath the inflated padding of the sleeping bag that was pulled tight around his neck.

Chisnall took a step closer and used his weapon to loosen the top of the sleeping bag. There was a sudden chafing noise, like two pieces of fabric rubbing together. He lifted it higher and an olive-green snake with black checkered scales appeared at the mouth of the bag, raising its head as if to attack before slithering quickly over the rocks and down toward the river.

The hard man of the refugee camps had been no match for a creature of the Australian desert.

"Damn! Inland taipan," Brogan said. "Deadliest snake in the world."

"Unlucky dude," Wilton said.

"You think?" Price said.

"From now on, everybody check your sleeping bags before you crawl into them," Brogan said. "We don't want anyone else to get unlucky."

There was a murmur of agreement from the others.

Unlucky was right, Chisnall thought. But not for the reason that they thought. Seven of the deadliest snakes in the world live in Australia. But this was too much of a coincidence, especially after the sabotaged half-pipe. And the inland taipan might be the deadliest snake in the world, but it was also one of the shyest. It did not attack unless threatened, and the chances of one crawling into Hunter's sleeping bag were slim. And why hadn't Hunter cried out? A taipan's bite was deadly, but death was not instantaneous. The only reason Chisnall could think of was that Hunter had already been unconscious when he had been bitten.

But why? Had Hunter seen or heard something? Had he interrupted the traitor in another act? If so, what was it?

"Bury him," he said. "And his gear. Except for the laser comm. Brogan, you take that. And eat your breakfast. We are Oscar Mike in twenty."

Brogan extracted the laser comm unit from Hunter's backpack while the rest of them prepared a hole in the sand. Chisnall recorded the GPS coordinates of the grave. That was standard practice behind enemy lines, in case there was ever an opportunity in the future to recover the body.

"LT." It was Brogan.

"What is it?" Chisnall asked.

"The laser comm, it's nonfunctional."

"Let me have a look," Chisnall said.

He knelt down beside her and examined the unit. It powered up okay, but when he pressed the test switch, the diagnostic lights glowed red instead of green. He shook it a couple of times in case there was just something loose inside it, but the unit refused to work.

"Sh-shoot," he said, slamming a hand into the desert floor. Sand sprayed in all directions. "Shoot, shoot, shoot!" Without the laser comm, they had no way of communicating with their base. He took a deep breath to calm himself. Displays of emotion like that helped nobody.

"What do we do, LT?" Brogan asked.

"Bring it anyway. Maybe it'll start working again."

He doubted that would happen, just as he doubted that it was a coincidence that it had stopped working. Under cover of the sandstorm, someone had sabotaged the single most important piece of equipment they carried. Hunter must have had his suspicions. Maybe he'd caught them in the act, and the result of that was the snake in his sleeping bag. Chisnall mentally kicked himself. If only he'd taken the time to listen to Hunter earlier.

"Jeez, Ryan," Brogan said, shaking her head. "We can't carry on now. Even if we find something, we won't be able to let base know what we've found."

"Just get moving," Chisnall said.

"Seriously, LT, perhaps we should ease up for a bit," Brogan said. "Most of these guys have never even seen a dead body before, let alone someone they know. A friend of theirs. They might need a little time to get their heads around it."

"My orders are to proceed to Uluru without delay," Chisnall said.

She shook her head slowly. "Hunter just died. Don't you feel anything?"

He did. That was the problem.

"It doesn't matter what I feel," he said.

"Ryan, I know what happened in Bering Strait," she said. "But—"

Chisnall stood and eyeballed her. "Don't go there, *Sergeant* Brogan," he said. "You asked. I answered. We are Oscar Mike in twenty. Get him buried. Deep, so the dingoes don't get him."

Specialist Stephen Huntington was sixteen.

He was the first Angel to die.

5. BENDA HILL

[MISSION DAY 5]
[0100 hours]
[Benda Hill, New Bzadia]

THE AMBUSH HAPPENED ON THE LAST DAY OF THEIR HIKE, as they were passing Benda Hill.

After three nights of tabbing, Chisnall was moving more easily, the ragged agony of his back and legs now just a dull, constant throb.

The desert here was vastly different from the scarred hill-sides of Mount Morris or the long furrowed dunes of the southern desert. It was flat, and the ground was hard. Had he landed on the semi-inflated half-pipe in this part of the desert, he would not have survived. Benda Hill was a large, rounded knob of rock, protruding from the desert plane. Gray by daylight but green in their NV goggles. The sides looked smooth but the top was pitted and creviced by millions of years of harsh Australian weather.

The loss of Hunter had affected the entire team. Chisnall could feel it. All the training in the world could not prepare you for the first time you lost a comrade.

"Damn this war," Wilton said, surprising them all with his vehemence. "Damn it. I'm sixteen: I should be shredding the backcountry at Whistler, not busting a gut humping a pack through this hellhole, surrounded by deadly snakes and butt-ugly aliens who want to kill me."

"I know it," Price agreed. "I should be hanging out behind the pub, scrounging old cigarette butts out of the sand trays while my dad's getting smashed inside and my mum is pouring the housekeeping into the pokies."

"Does anyone here speak Kiwi?" Wilton asked.

Chisnall shook his head. "I have no idea what she said."

It was Brogan who seemed to understand, resting her hand lightly on Price's shoulder. "That was home?"

"Nothing ever changes," Price said.

"Damn this war," Wilton said again.

"How about you, Monster?" Chisnall asked.

"My dudes, if not for the war, the Monster would be drinking beer with his buddies until he couldn't see straight." His booming laugh filled the desert around them.

"You can't drink beer; you're only sixteen," Brogan said.

"I drank some beer once," Price said. "Didn't like it much."

"Me too," Wilton said. "At least I think it was beer."

"The Monster is from Röszke, just over the border from

Serbia." Monster looked around and grinned at them. "In Serbia there is no, how do you say, you are old enough for drinking?"

"Legal drinking age," Chisnall said.

"Aha, legal drinking age. So kids walk to bars in Horgoš and roll all the way back home." That laugh sounded so loud that Chisnall began to worry how far it would carry in the desert.

"You ever do that, Monster?" Price asked. "Get drunk in Horgoš?"

"Pukes invaded Hungary in '26. He'd have been, like, twelve," Brogan said.

Monster nodded. "The Monster was eleven when my family became refugees. America won't allow the Monster to drink beer till he's twenty-one."

"Good thing too," Price said. "You're crazy enough when you're sober."

"How about you, LT?" Wilton asked. "What would you be doing right now, if not for the war?"

"Sleeping," Chisnall said.

"Other than that," Wilton said.

"I don't know," Chisnall said. "I never got the chance to figure that out."

"That isn't what you told me," Brogan said.

"Now you gotta tell us," Price said.

"I'm the LT," Chisnall said. "I don't gotta do nothing."

"So you tell us, Sarge," Wilton said.

"Sergeant Brogan, I am sure you wouldn't breach the

confidentiality of a discussion between an officer and an NCO," Chisnall said.

"Of course not, LT," Brogan said. "These lowlifes are just going to have to wait until you're a famous TV chef before they find out."

"TV chef!" Wilton burst out laughing.

"Oops," Brogan said.

"I never said TV," Chisnall said.

"I heard it," Brogan said.

"So why you serve us green crap for meals?" Monster asked. "Can't a chef do better than that?"

"Especially a famous TV chef," Price said.

Chisnall sighed. "Look . . . when I was a kid, before we got recruited—"

"Serves you right for being so good at paintball," Brogan said.

"If I'd known that it meant getting recruited, I'd have missed every shot," Wilton said.

"Carry on, LT," Price said. "I gotta hear this."

"Well . . . you know. I was into cooking," Chisnall said.

"We'd be good friends." Monster laughed. "The Monster is into eating."

"I just loved the way you could take a few raw ingredients and add a bit of heat and end up with something completely different," Chisnall said. "It's a kind of magic. I always thought I'd like to go to cooking school and learn how to do it properly."

"Sounds really gay to me," Wilton said, and got a shove in his back from Brogan for his trouble.

"No, really, I'm just saying," he said.

"Yeah, and what were you planning to do with your life, Wilton?" Price asked. "Professional snow-bunny? Maybe a snowboard instructor, getting hit on by the arctic cougars in the après-ski?"

"Shut up," Wilton said.

"I wonder what Hunter's dreams were," Price said, and the chill of the night air grew suddenly colder, an icy blanket drawing around them.

"He never even got to fire a shot," Wilton said.

There was a moment's silence.

"The Pukes are going to pay for Hunter," Monster said.

"Booyah," Price said.

"Here we come, you alien mother-shippers," Wilton said. "You want some of this, Pukes? Come get some. I got enough kick-ass for all you vomit bags."

"Booyah," Price said again.

"Wilton," Chisnall said. "We're a recon team. We're not shock troops. If we go in screaming and shooting, that's pretty much going to screw up our mission, don't you think?"

Wilton seemed not to have heard him. "My dad took out two Puke LAVs with one rocket during the defense of Okinawa. He just about won the battle by himself."

"I don't know if you got the memo, Wilton," Brogan said, "but we lost Okinawa."

"Two LAVs! One rocket. Right down the ammo hatch. Goes up like the Fourth of July. Boom! Blows the one next to it right off the road. Over a cliff. *Boom, boom, boom,* all the way down."

"Buy one, get one free," Monster said.

"Guys," Chisnall said. "Guys, seriously. Listen up. No more talking about killing Pukes. We're in the heart of Puke country now. We've got to start acting and thinking like Pukes. Everything you say, everything you do from now on, you're a Puke. You want to pick your nose, use two thumbs at once, like they do. You want to scratch your ass, don't. Pukes see you do that, they'll spot you for a fraud from a klick away."

"Don't Pukes ever get an itchy arse?" Monster asked.

"If they do," Brogan said, "they're polite enough not to scratch them in public."

"Gonna scratch their asses right off our planet," Wilton said.

"Our planet?" Brogan asked.

"Hell yeah, our planet," Wilton said.

"How'd you figure that?" Brogan said. "Pukes control Australia, Africa, Europe, and most of Asia. We've got the Americas."

"We still got Antarctica," Price said.

"Only 'cause they don't want it. I figure we have less than forty percent of the Earth's landmass. Which gives the Pukes over sixty percent. It seems to me that if this planet belongs to anyone now, it belongs to them."

"Piss off," Price said. "It was ours in the first place."

"And after the white folk conquered the American Indians, who got to run the country and who got to live on reservations?" Brogan asked.

"You're saying the Pukes are going to make us live on reservations?" Wilton asked.

"If we're lucky," Brogan said. "It's just evolution, that's all."

"What are you talking about?" Wilton asked. "How is it evolution?"

"We used to be just a bunch of flea-bitten monkeys living in trees and scratching around in the dirt like all the other animals," Brogan said. "We weren't very big or strong, but we got smart, and soon we were the top of the food chain. Top of the pecking order. But not anymore. Now there's someone else at the top of the food chain, and we don't like it."

"Guys," Chisnall said. "You need to—"

The first burst of gunfire must have been well above their heads, but the whistle of bullets in the air sounded as though they were right by their ears.

"Contact front!" Price yelled.

Chisnall's instincts took over. His combat visor was down, his coil-gun in his hands, before he had even formed a conscious thought. He rolled to the right, seeking cover behind a boulder. He scanned the desert ahead of his position, looking for movement.

"Muzzle flashes, one o'clock," Brogan yelled.

There shouldn't have been muzzle flashes. The magnetically powered coil-guns did not flash like human weapons, and alien gunfire did not sound like the explosions of cordite; the rounds broke the sound barrier on their way out of the barrel. This gunfire sounded and looked like an assault rifle. A human weapon.

The others had also dived for rocks or scrub, whatever they could find. Chisnall stuck his head above the rock for a second to try and spot their position and was rewarded with another burst of fire. Chips of rock exploded from the top of the boulder right in front of him. From the sound of the firing and the way the rock fragments had flown, he had a pretty good idea of the location of the shooters. He shucked his backpack off his shoulders.

"Covering fire," he yelled into the comm, and immediately was encased in a cocoon of sound as his team responded with a hail of shots. They were firing wildly, but the targets didn't know that, so it should keep their heads down for a moment.

Chisnall rolled sideways out from the cover of the rock and onto his feet in one fluid motion, sprinting to a sloping rocky shelf a few feet away. He reached it just as return gunfire rang out from the other side, and bullets *zizz*ed through the air around him.

"Anyone got eyes on them?" he said softly into the comm.

Brogan replied immediately. "Cluster of boulders at the base of the hill."

"How many guns?" Chisnall asked, training the night-sight of his weapon on that location. Here, behind the rocky shelf, he had a good field of fire without exposing himself to the shooters. He caught a slight movement, a vague dark shape behind the boulders.

"Only one, maybe two," Brogan said.

"Strange," Chisnall said. "It's not big enough for a patrol."

"Why the hell are they using MP5s?" Brogan asked.

[0110 hours]

[Perimeter Fence, Uluru Military Base, New Bzadia]

Kezalu stopped singing.

Yozi glanced up at him. They had been scouting the perimeter fence for two hours and Kezalu had been singing for most of it. Yozi wasn't sure if Kezalu even realized he was doing it. He had a fine, clear, young voice, and the others in his squad had long since learned to tune it out.

Kezalu was on the fifty-caliber machine gun, mounted high on the Australian Army Land Rover. It was one of the few human weapons they actually used. Most Earth weapons were so primitive, heavy, and underpowered that they were not worth bothering with. But the big fifty-cal, although huge and unwieldy, fired such large projectiles that they could punch through body armor, vehicles, even buildings. And the weight of the weapon was not an issue if it was rack-mounted on top of a vehicle.

The Land Rovers were primitive, internal-combustion vehicles, and nobody much liked them. They had appropriated hundreds of them from the Australian Army when they had sent it running, however, and they were well suited to the rough desert terrain.

Kezalu had been singing a song from his homeland, the kind of song that only a young, innocent soldier, straight out of basic training, would sing. In some squads it would be seen as a sign of weakness, and the other soldiers would have beaten it out of him after the first day. But Yozi did not hold with that, and the members of his squad knew it, so they left Kezalu alone.

But Kezalu had stopped singing. He cocked his head to one side, as if listening.

"Stop the engine," Yozi murmured to Zabet, the driver.

She complied immediately, flicking the Land Rover into neutral and letting it coast slowly to a halt. Yozi twisted around in the oversized (human-sized) chair and signaled Alizza in the Land Rover behind them to do the same.

Kezalu took off his helmet, listening. This time, without the rumble of the noisy engine, Yozi heard it too. They all did.

The sound of gunfire. The short popping sound of coilguns answered by the hard cracking noise of a machine gun.

A human weapon.

Yozi aimed a flat hand in the direction he thought it was coming from and looked up at Kezalu. Kezalu shook his head and aimed his own hand slightly to the left of Yozi's.

"Call it in," Yozi said.

Zabet nodded and reached for the comm.

■ ■ ■

Wilton was hammering away on his coil-gun, laying down a constant stream of fire that would use up his entire ammo supply in a few minutes if he didn't slow down.

"Cease fire, cease fire," Chisnall called, and the firing stopped.

Echoes of the noise seemed to be rebounding off the big rocky hillside in front of him, but he knew that was just his ears adjusting to the sudden silence of the desert.

There was a short burst from the boulders in front of them.

"MP5s, are you sure?" Chisnall asked.

"I'm sure."

"Hey, scumbugzzz," he called out in English, but in his best Bzadian accent. "Hey, scumbugzzz. Stop you shooting, yezzz."

The voice that came back was unmistakably English.

"Lay your weapons on the ground and raise your hands above your heads. We have you surrounded."

No, you don't, Chisnall thought. *Not with just one or two of you.*

"I coming out, yezzz," he called out, and then said quietly on the comm, "I don't think they're Pukes."

"Careful, LT," said Brogan in his ear. "It could be a trap."

"Phantom, you know what to do," Chisnall said.

He raised his weapon high above his head and stepped out from behind the rock.

There were no shots.

He walked forward, keeping the coil-gun above his head, then unclipped it from the holster spring and slowly laid it on the ground. He did the same for his sidearm and advanced toward the boulders, keeping his hands high.

"That's close enough, thanks," the voice called. "Now the other chaps."

Chisnall dropped the accent. "Who the hell are you, soldier?"

"There's a platoon of us," the voice said.

"No, there isn't," Chisnall said. "There are two or three of you at the most, and if there was a platoon in this vicinity, I'd know about it."

"Who are you?"

"Lieutenant Ryan Chisnall, Allied Combined Operations Group, Recon Battalion," Chisnall said.

"You look like a Puke," the voice said.

"I'm no more Puke than you are," Chisnall said. "Good disguise, though, yezz?"

"Keep your hands on top of your head," the voice said. "And come behind the boulders."

Chisnall walked forward slowly, making no movements that might alarm the men. He stepped between two of the boulders.

There were just two of them, one injured. Both in their twenties or early thirties. Both in the uniform of the British Royal Air Force. They had just one weapon between them, an MP5. Brogan was right.

"Dammit, you really are a Puke," the man said as Chisnall rounded the rocks. He aimed the gun at Chisnall's face.

"No, I'm not," Chisnall said. He flipped up his combat visor.

"You damn well look like one," the man said. "Tell your men to lay their weapons on the ground and come over here."

"They're already here," Chisnall said with an even smile.

"G'day, mate," Price said from behind the men.

The man looked around at the gun next to his head. Price, the Kiwi Phantom, had used Chisnall's approach as a cover to slither silently around behind them. Nobody had heard her—not even Chisnall, who knew what she was doing.

Chisnall reached forward and took the MP5 off the soldier, flipping the safety as the other Angels approached.

"Believe it or not, we are humans," he said. "I'm from California."

"Well, you look like Pukes."

"Believe me, we ain't happy about that either," Wilton said.

"Who are you?" Chisnall asked.

"Pilot Officer Sean Fleming. This is Flight Lieutenant Theo Bennett, Royal Air Force, Sixty-First Squadron."

The injured man nodded but did not speak.

"What's your story?" Chisnall asked.

The team squatted down in a semicircle around the two men.

"We were part of the raid on Townsville. Got chased by the Pukes halfway across Australia. They winged us and we managed to eject, but the skipper landed on rocks, banged up his leg a bit. We've been evading ever since."

"Any plans to get you out?" Brogan asked.

Fleming shook his head. "If we could get to the coast, maybe, but there's not much chance of that with the skipper's leg. How about you? What are you doing here?"

"That's classified," Chisnall said.

Fleming nodded. "I thought as much. Five kids dressed as Pukes in the heart of Puke land."

Chisnall turned to Brogan. "I want to debrief these men on enemy activity in the area. Retrieve the backpacks and set up a perimeter. Full alert. Pukes may have heard the shooting."

Chisnall waited until the others had vanished into the darkness of the desert, then shook Fleming's hand warmly. He made sure his comm mike was off.

"The uniform looks good on you." He grinned.

"I think so too," Fleming said. "How'd I do?"

"Convincing. You almost had me fooled."

"Good to see you again, kid," Fleming said. He winced. "Sorry, I know you hate being called that."

"Don't worry about it. Good to see you too. But what the hell was all that shooting as we approached the RV?"

"There were supposed to be six of you," Fleming said. "We thought you were a real patrol, and you were just about to walk over the top of us."

"Just as well you SAS guys can't hit the side of a barn at ten paces with a shotgun," Chisnall said.

"If we'd been aiming at you, you would have known all about it," Fleming said. "I fired high in case it was you."

"You just about took my head off by that boulder," Chisnall said.

"Only because you stuck it up at exactly the wrong time," Fleming said.

"Where's Hunter?" Bennett asked, speaking for the first time. He was clearly in pain.

"He's dead. Snakebite," Chisnall answered.

"The desert is a dangerous place," Bennett said.

"Yeah, and not just the wildlife," Chisnall said.

Bennett looked closely at him. "It wasn't an accident?"

"I doubt it." Chisnall told them about the laser comm unit and the half-pipe.

"Any idea who did it?" Bennett's voice was low and dangerous.

"None," Chisnall said. "And it was done under cover of a sandstorm so the satellites wouldn't see."

"Tricky," Fleming said.

"Are you still go for the mission, with the leg?"

"It's not as bad as it looks, Lieutenant. I'll be okay. Besides, it'll add authenticity," Bennett said.

"No problems avoiding the Pukes?" Chisnall asked.

"They know we're here, somewhere," Fleming said. "They've been looking high and low."

"Yeah, we saw a lot of search activity," Chisnall said.

"They haven't found us yet." Fleming grinned.

"Good," Chisnall said. "What time are the fireworks?"

"I'll call it in now," Fleming said. He opened a small satchel and took out a laser comm unit, identical to the one Hunter had carried. "The carrier group is already in position."

"Any danger to us?" Chisnall asked.

Bennett shook his head. "We're well outside the fire zone."

"Okay. After you've called it in, bury the laser comm. Don't let my guys see it."

Bennett nodded. "We won't be needing it again."

"LT." It was Price's voice on the comm.

"Copy," Chisnall said, turning his comm mike back on.

"I think we've got company. A slow mover just broke off from the activity up around Uluru. Heading this way. Someone must have heard the shooting."

Chisnall looked to the north. There was nothing visible in the sky.

"How long have we got?" he asked.

"Maybe ten mikes, if we're lucky."

"Copy that. Brogan, get the team up the hill. Cover all approaches. Camo down, and no movement unless I give the word."

He didn't say it out loud, but the success of the mission depended on them not getting spotted. For a few more hours at least.

"Clear copy, LT," Brogan said.

"Will you be okay getting up there?" Chisnall asked Bennett.

The hill was steep, although there was a more gradual slope on the northern face.

"I'll be fine, but I think it's a bad idea," Bennett said.

Chisnall glanced around. "There's nowhere else that's defendable. The hill would give us height advantage and good fields of fire if they do find us."

Bennett shook his head. "Too exposed. A couple of mortar rounds and we'd be dingo food. Just tell your team to spread out and camo down."

"Sir, no, sir."

"You realize you are talking to a colonel."

"Yes, sir."

"I was running combat operations against the Pukes when you were still a twinkle in your daddy's eye."

"That's probably not true, sir. And I have mission command."

Fleming said, "The kid has good instincts, Colonel. And we don't have time to argue."

Bennett said, "Okay, looks like you're in charge, Lieutenant."

Chisnall nodded. He hoped he wasn't making another huge mistake.

6. ULURU

[0240 hours]
[Benda Hill, New Bzadia]

ULURU BY NIGHT HAD A PHYSICAL PRESENCE, EVEN though it was little more than a dark, distant mass against the star-scattered sky. It was easy to see why the Aboriginal people revered it. Folklore had it that anyone who removed as much as a stone from Uluru would be cursed. The aliens had been burrowing into Uluru for years. If the story was true, then the Bzadians were in for the mother of all curses.

Chisnall hoped it was true.

Uluru might have been dark and silent but the land around it was quite the opposite. From the top of the hill, Chisnall's binoculars picked up a blaze of lights in the mass of encampments, barracks, supply stores, and defenses around the rock. Roads were lined with lights and a monorail ran in a wide circle around the rock before disappearing into a cleft in the rock face.

A constant stream of trucks and smaller vehicles flowed on the roadways around the big rock. Uluru remained almost invisible, except when one of the rotorcraft passed over it, the craft's downlights creating a vivid red burst of sandstone in the blackness.

In between their hill and Uluru was a massive electrified fence, topped by a long line of lights, deadly sparkling baubles. Outside the fence was a minefield. A secondary, smaller fence ran outside that, no doubt to stop any patrols or animals from wandering into the mines. Inside the main fence were the heavy concrete pyramids called dragon's teeth: tank traps. At fifty-meter intervals were concrete towers with narrow slots at the top. Each one held a heavy-caliber coil-gun linked to a motion sensor. Cameras on the top of the towers covered every angle. The only way in or out was through the gate stations on the western and eastern approaches to Uluru. And outside the smaller fence, dead kangaroos and dingoes—just large enough to trigger the automatic guns—rotted where they had fallen.

The place was impregnable.

Chisnall tried to bury his face in the rock, holding his breath as the enemy rotorcraft hovered overhead. He used his hands and feet to hold the straps on each corner of the camo sheet to prevent it from moving or flapping in the heavy downdraft from the rotor blades.

The top of Benda Hill was a ragged jumble of rocks and

crevices—natural foxholes that offered almost perfect cover against an attack.

A gunship, bristling with heavy weapons and rocket pods, had flown over the hill but had not detected the Angel Team or the British soldiers.

Chisnall checked the time. They had been hiding under their camo sheets for more than two hours. The Pukes were still searching. Most of their activity had concentrated on a scrubby area southwest of Benda Hill. That area offered many places to hide, and the Pukes had turned it over with a fine-tooth comb. Like Bennett, the Pukes seemed to have regarded the top of the hill as too exposed and had ignored it.

Until now.

The craft hovered above them, its electronic eyes—and the eyes of its crew—examining the top of the hill minutely.

"I think they've rumbled us," Brogan said quietly on the comm.

The gunship moved slowly away, holding off about a hundred meters.

Chisnall opened his mouth to say something else but never got the chance. The front edge of the craft dipped as it accelerated into attack mode. There was a series of flashes from the rocket pods on either side of the cockpit and the hilltop was engulfed in a thunderstorm of sound and fury. Pulverized rock flew into the air and waves of concussion blasted through the rocky ridges. Chisnall hugged the floor in a steep-sided crevice and saw wedges of rock flying above his head. He fought for breath and heard a cry of agony over the comm.

Another wave of rockets lashed the hilltop, then another. Only the jagged crevices of the rock saved them from the percussive blasts. The rotorcraft lifted its nose into the air and headed away, back to its base.

"They're withdrawing!" Wilton yelled. "Booyah!"

"Watch the scope, watch the scope!" Chisnall yelled.

"Here they come," Price called. "Two fast movers heading our way."

"They'll take out the entire hill," Brogan said.

"Get out of here, now!" Chisnall yelled. "Over the back!"

It was the only option he could see. To get down on the opposite side of the hill from the approaching jets.

"Three klicks out," Price called.

Bennett appeared close to him, and Chisnall grabbed his arm, helping him limp across the ragged hilltop. Bennett was heavy and much larger than Chisnall and the going was slow.

"Two klicks."

Fleming appeared on the other side of Bennett and the three of them stumbled toward the southern end of the rock.

"One klick!"

The hill dropped away and they scrambled and fell through a patch of porcupine grass, the needles stabbing at any exposed skin. Then the ground beneath their feet disappeared completely and they were falling over a small bluff.

They hit another steep slope hard and were sliding and rolling. Chisnall crashed into a tree halfway down and stopped there, winded, as Bennett and Fleming continued sliding past him. Above him, the hilltop exploded into a massive ball of flame, sucking all the oxygen out of the air. Huge orbs of flame streaked with charcoal leaped into the night air. Benda Hill erupted like a volcano. The land around it turned orange, then yellow, bathing in the fiery anger of the hilltop above.

"Angel Team, status check," Chisnall gasped into the comm.

"Angel Two. Oscar Kilo."

"Angel Four. Oscar Kilo."

"Angel Five, I took a shrapnel hit from the rocket attack, but the body armor held. I'm Oscar Kilo."

"Angel Six. Oscar Kilo."

Chisnall scrambled down the hillside to Fleming and Bennett. Both were breathing heavily and blood was seeping from a deep gash on Fleming's face.

"You guys okay?" Chisnall asked.

"I don't think that did my leg any favors," Bennett said. "But I'm no worse off than I was before."

Fleming just nodded. He found a gauze pad and held it firmly to the gash on his face.

"Is that all you got?" Wilton yelled at the sky.

"Price, what are those fast movers doing?" Chisnall asked.

"Looks like they're coming back for more," she said.

[0450 hours]

[New Bzadian Early Warning Radar Center, Uluru Military Base, New Bzadia]

Inzusu watched the jets on his radar as they wheeled around.

Of all the jobs in the Bzadian Army, his had to be the most boring, but by that definition, also one of the safest. For which Inzusu was grateful. Not for him the terror of combat on the front line.

This was the most excitement he had had since starting this job. Human jets over New Bzadia. Intruders within striking distance of the base.

Lozpe was his supervisor today. Inzusu didn't like him much and fortunately rarely saw him, as Lozpe was the kind who supervised from his office with his head on his desk. He rarely ventured out onto the radar floor, unlike Czali, who was constantly pacing, moving from one screen to another.

Right now, however, Lozpe was hovering right next to Inzusu, watching the jets lining up their next attack run.

A subtle change in the light patterns on the very fringe of his radar drew Inzusu's eyes in that direction. A smattering of dots. At first he thought it was interference or maybe a chaff cloud, because the pattern was so dense and so widespread.

The radar system clearly thought so too. Its basic intelligence struggled to define the strange signal. What did it mean? The fuzzy signal moved closer, resolving itself from a cloud to a series of distinct dots. Thousands of them. So many that the analysis computer was struggling to identify and deal with each one individually. There was a pause as the system interrogated the airspace and waited for a response from any aircraft in that area.

Nothing came.

Inzusu was starting to get alarmed now, although the radar had not yet identified the dots as a threat.

His brain and the signal analysis computer both set off warning bells at the same time.

None of the signals was broadcasting an identification code.

They were enemy aircraft.

"Azoh!"

His hand hit the alarm button by the side of his keyboard even as he felt Lozpe's breath on the back on his neck.

"What is it? What have you got?" Lozpe asked, not yet registering the cloud pattern at the top of the screen.

"Enemy aircraft inbound," Inzusu said, his voice barely a whisper.

"Where?" Lozpe seemed confused. "What are they throwing at us today?"

Inzusu pointed to the fuzzy mass at the top of the screen. "Everything," he said.

Chisnall could see the Bzadian fast movers in the distance, arcs of light in the sky, circling around for another attack.

"Bring it on," Wilton roared.

Chisnall searched desperately around them. They were out in the open now, with no chance of evasion and no cover. Sitting ducks.

"Wait!" Price's voice. "They're peeling off."

"You're sure?" Chisnall asked.

"Why?" Brogan asked.

Chisnall said nothing, his eyes fixed on the darkened night sky. The troop carrier was bugging out as well.

The air defenses around Uluru exploded into life.

"What the hell?" Brogan said.

"The raid," Chisnall said. "It's started."

"What raid?" Brogan asked.

"Let's get back up the hill," Chisnall said. "I want a ticket to this show."

They worked their way around to the gentle northern slope of Benda Hill and back up to the top. Their former defensive positions were now crumbled, blackened rock. They had got out just in time.

Bzadian fast movers were streaming in from the east and west to meet the threat from the north, and there were constant flashes in the sky above them.

"They're too small to be fighters," Inzusu said. His fingers flicked over the display, spinning it, zooming it. "They're drones, probably predators."

"How many planes have we got up against them?" Lozpe asked.

"Not enough," Inzusu said. He watched the screen for another few seconds. It was alive with swarms of Bzadian defenders moving to intercept the intruders. Missiles were flying in both directions. He saw two defenders get hit simultaneously and tumble from the sky. The predators were firing antiair. That was unusual.

Surface-to-air missile (SAM) sites around Uluru lit up. Inzusu glanced at one of the live-cam feeds. He saw fiery lines streak up into the sky as the SAMs engaged the enemy, but there were matching streaks of lightning emerging from the sky and tracing back down the path of the SAMs.

Every time a SAM battery fired, it gave away its position, and the scumbugz had advanced anti-SAMs. The SAM batteries had to keep moving constantly to avoid becoming a target.

He could feel the concussions now, vibrating through the ground as missiles impacted above their heads.

"Wait a minute," he said, his eyes flicking between the radar screen and the analysis readouts.

"What is it?" Lozpe asked. When Inzusu didn't immediately answer, he repeated the question. "What is it?"

"It's all antiair and anti-SAM," Inzusu said. "Everything. The entire attack is aimed at our defensive aircraft screen and our SAM sites. They're not attacking any other ground installations."

"Which means?"

"They're softening us up."

He reached for the radio but got only static. He looked at Lozpe in horror. "They've jammed our comms."

"And our radar." Lozpe seemed dazed, as if shocked by the speed and scale of what he was seeing.

Inzusu turned back to the radar screen in time to see a cloud of white noise descend over it, blocking all the signals. The enemy was systematically destroying their defenses and jamming the radar and communications.

That could mean only one thing.

A glow in the sky ahead of them grew rapidly larger and turned into a Bzadian jet—a big one, a type two. It was heading straight for them, its wings on fire.

It passed so low overhead that they could feel its heat before it crashed and sent up a fireball in the desert to the south.

"Booyah," Wilton said quietly.

Ahead of them, the sky was alive with the constant thunderclap of explosions.

A faint noise was flicking at Chisnall's ears. He turned his head slightly and was greeted by a sudden roaring sound and a blast of air.

"What the—" Brogan said.

It was a missile. Ground hugging, to avoid radar. It streaked past the hill they were on at such a low altitude that they were actually looking down on it as it passed.

What kind it was, Chisnall couldn't tell. The speed at which it was traveling meant that it was no more than a rush of air and a streak of light, followed a few seconds later by a massive, screeching explosion and billowing flame from the north.

"Take that!" Chisnall yelled.

An entire submarine fleet had been dodging icebergs in the Southern Ocean in complete radio silence and full stealth mode. A few days earlier, the group had turned north and quietly made their way toward the coast of Australia. Waiting for the signal.

Another missile passed them, and another, and suddenly the air around the hill seemed alive with massive insects attracted to the heat and light of the burning base at Uluru.

It was a fireworks show like none that had ever been seen before. It seemed unearthly and weird to be sitting high on a rock as the missiles streaked past below them.

Tomahawks, Exocets, Silkworms, Russian Granat missiles, and more. They honed in on the now largely undefended Uluru military base. With the alien fast movers busy engaging the predators and the SAM sites relocating or being destroyed, the missiles approaching from the south were relatively unimpeded.

Then came the second wave.

And the third.

The ground itself seemed to be flexing and undulating.

The desert was on fire.

Not all the missiles were accurate. A number fell short, in a series of explosions that rippled across the twin fences and the defenses of the outer perimeter.

"What the hell is going on?" Wilton asked.

"We're sending them a message," Chisnall said.

"Booyah," Monster said.

Up to now, Earth forces had been on the run, fighting defensive actions, trying to hold back the unstoppable Puke army. Now, for the first time, Allied forces were taking the fight to the Pukes, striking deep in the heart of New Bzadia, at their biggest military installation.

"Yeah, now get the hell off our planet," Wilton said, but his voice was low and subdued. Even he was shocked by the sheer volume of the ordnance that was raining down in front of their eyes.

"You knew about this raid in advance," Brogan said in a slightly accusatory tone as they scraped their way back down the northern slope of Benda Hill.

"I know lots of things that you don't know," Chisnall said. "That's why I'm the leader."

"Anything else you want to share?" Brogan asked.

"Nope."

"Thought not."

At the base of the hill, behind the clump of boulders, the Angels squatted in a circle and Chisnall consulted his GPS tablet.

"Okay, here it is," Chisnall said. "The big raid is our cover."

"They put on this whole show just for us?" Monster said. "Cheese and rice!"

"No, not just for us," Chisnall said. "But with all the confusion and destruction, we should be able to get in relatively easily. They'll have plenty on their minds without double-checking ID from every grunt in the field. The missiles took out a large section of the fence and the minefield. That's our welcome mat."

"You'd think someone would have mentioned this at the mission briefing," Brogan said.

Chisnall stowed the tablet and looked around the team. "Up till two days ago, less than three people in the world knew about this raid. Some people knew parts of it, for planning and coordination, but almost nobody had all the parts of the jigsaw. And the target was under wraps until yesterday. Most of those involved in the planning thought they were attacking a base in Singapore."

"Why all the secrecy?" Price asked. "Don't nobody trust nobody no more?"

"Something like that," Chisnall said. "My orders were to tell no one until the raid began. If the Pukes had found out about this, it would have been a disaster for our side. But right now is the best chance any human has ever had to get inside Uluru and find out what they're up to. So let's not hang around here gossiping all day."

"Booyah!" Wilton said.

"What about the RAF guys?" Brogan asked.

"They're coming with us," Chisnall said.

"What?" Price said.

"You're nuts, LT," Brogan said. "No offense, skipper, but on this you're nuts. We can pass ourselves off as Pukes, but they can't."

"We'll treat them as our prisoners," Chisnall said. "It'll give us extra credibility. Once we're inside the base, they can hide out somewhere, until we're ready to leave. Then our extraction team can pick them up as well."

"How exactly are we being extracted from this mission?" Brogan asked. "That part I'm not quite clear on."

"Sorry, Brogan," Chisnall said.

"That's above your security level," Price said with a roll of her eyes.

"Right now we need to get moving. Oscar Mike in five. From now on, you don't just act like Pukes—you *are* Pukes. We're going right inside their biggest military base."

"Into belly of beast," Monster said.

Wilton and Price dug a deep hole, into which went their camo sheets and other non-Bzadian items. Then with Monster on point and Fleming helping Bennett walk, they started the last part of their trek. Chisnall walked at the rear, watching them.

Five teenage recon soldiers.

Two SAS troopers disguised as RAF officers.

One traitor.

Across the flat scrubby desert of central Australia.

Past the twisted, ruined wire of the security fences and remains of the gun towers.

Toward Uluru.

BOOK 2—THE BASE

7. BELLY OF BEAST

[MISSION DAY 5]
[0530 hours]
[Benda Hill, New Bzadia]

THE WRECKAGE OF THE INNER FENCE WAS A TANGLED metal cobweb lying across the remains of the dragon's-teeth tank traps.

"Land mine," Price said over the top of an insistent beeping from her scope.

Chisnall stopped dead. They all did. They were walking in single file, four meters apart, treading in the footprints of the person in front. Standard precautions for walking through a minefield.

Except there shouldn't have been any land mines. The cruise missiles had ripped through here, pummeling the desert floor, punching a hole through this section of the defenses.

The churned sand of the desert should have been cleared of mines by the rippling shock waves of the explosions.

"Are you sure?" Chisnall asked, but only as an automatic reaction. Of course she was sure. She wouldn't have said it if she wasn't.

"Two o'clock. Distance: three meters," Price said. "And a bit."

"Three meters." Chisnall breathed out slowly.

The alien mines had proximity detectors. You didn't have to stand on them to set them off: if they detected movement within three meters, they would explode, kicking a shrapnel canister high into the air, killing or maiming everything around it.

They were just on the verge of triggering the mine.

"Back away slowly," Chisnall said.

"Good idea, LT," Price said. "Should have thought of that myself."

Chisnall ignored her. Things were tense enough. Price was already moving backward, retracing her steps.

"Options?" Chisnall asked.

"Looks clear to the left," Price said.

"Take it slowly," Chisnall said.

"You think?" Price said.

Twice more they found their path blocked by mines. One an antipersonnel mine and one an antitank mine. They were unlikely to set off the ATM, as it was keyed to large metallic objects, but they avoided it anyway. The explosive power of the ATMs was enormous, although they were not as deadly.

Not to humans anyway. The charge was focused straight upward, without the shrapnel spread pattern of the anti-personnel mines.

They moved through the main fence and past the pulverized base of one of the guard towers. Its automatic coil-guns whirred and clicked, sensing their presence, but the bent, broken snouts just shook angry fingers at the sky.

In the distance, Uluru glowed red: a warning beacon in the early morning sun.

The two SAS men, in their RAF disguises, walked silently in front of them, their hands manacled behind their backs.

"How far is it?" Wilton asked, eyeing the red rock behemoth in the distance. It was hard to judge scale in the desert.

"We're in the exclusion zone. It's about two hours of hard tabbing from here to the base itself," Chisnall said. "We want to get there while everything is still in chaos from the raid."

From this distance, chaos looked to be an understatement. A pall of smoke hung over Uluru from what must have been hundreds of fires, burning fiercely.

"Like the fires of Hades," Chisnall murmured.

"Call hell and tell them the Angels are coming," Brogan said.

"I just remembered that I have this really important appointment," Wilton said.

"Where's that?" Price asked.

"Anywhere," Wilton said. "Anywhere but here."

"Not me," Brogan said. "There's no place I'd rather be.

We've really hurt the Pukes for the first time, and this is our chance to stick the knife in."

"There's a whole lot of places I'd rather be," Price said.

"Yeah, like ten-buck-pizza Sundays at Hell's Kitchen," Wilton said.

"Mmmmm, pizza," Monster agreed. "Best food in the world!"

"I hate to break it to you," Chisnall said, "but there are better things in this world than melted cheese and processed meat on a bread-dough base."

"Mmmmm, pizza," Monster said again.

"The best thing in the world is not food," Wilton said. "It's when you're shredding down the monkey trails. That's beautiful, dude. That's better than sex."

"Like you'd know," Price said.

"I know more than you think," Wilton said, trying to look mysterious and not pulling it off.

"Really?" Price asked. "You ever even kissed a girl, Wilton?"

"Or a guy, whatever," Brogan said.

"Shut up," Wilton said.

"Didn't think so," Price said. "You want to know the best thing in the world? It's your first real kiss. You'll find out one day."

"Phantom, you've been reading too many romance novels," Chisnall said.

"I think I just puked in my mouth," Wilton said.

They arrived at the lip of an enormous crater where one

of the missiles had landed. It was wide but shallow, a quirk of the explosion and the geology of the underlying rock. Rather than skirt around it, Chisnall led the team down the soft, pulverized sand. Their boots slipped and skidded down the slope, creating mini landslides. The acrid after-smell of explosive was strong here. Parts of a tail fin protruded from the earth on the far side of the crater.

"What about you, Monster?" Brogan asked. "What do you think is the best thing in the world?"

"Well, my dude, the Monster thinks that nothing beats a really good fart."

There was a second's silence before the entire team burst into laughter.

"Evolution kinda skipped your family, didn't it?" Price said.

"So who wins?" Wilton asked. "Do we get to vote?"

"I'm not voting for Monster's fart," Price said.

"There's no voting," Chisnall said. "I get to pick the winner."

"Why's that?" Brogan asked.

"Because I'm the lieutenant," Chisnall said. "That's just the way it works. This is not a democracy."

"How come you're the LT?" Wilton asked. "You stronger or smarter than the rest of us?"

"No, Wilton, just better-looking," Chisnall said.

"Uh-uh, LT, you sho ain't purty," Wilton said. "Now, Sergeant Brogan, she's purty."

"You want some of this, soldier?" Brogan asked.

"If you bought me flowers and a nice dinner, I'd think about it," Wilton said.

Chisnall laughed. "I wouldn't if I were you. She'd chew you up and spit out the grisly bits for target practice."

"Wilton," Brogan said, "no offense, but I wouldn't feed you to my dog."

"Brogan," Wilton said, "do you ever wish you'd been born a boy?"

"No, how about you?" Brogan asked.

"Ground mobiles, ten o'clock," Price said. "Two of them. Small. Jeeps or Land Rovers. About three klicks out."

"Heading our way?" Chisnall asked.

"Not yet," Price said.

"Let's hope it stays that way," Chisnall said.

It didn't.

They were up out of the massive crater now. The light of the day was increasing with every minute and the clouds of dust from the vehicles were already visible without binoculars, rising in a red-gray plume to the northwest.

"They're turning," Price said. "Must have picked us up. Coming this way."

Chisnall took a deep breath. This was it. Contact with the enemy. This was what they had trained for. "Okay, everybody stay frosty," he said. "We're just a Puke patrol returning with some prisoners."

"Think they'll buy it?" Wilton asked.

"No reason why they shouldn't," Chisnall replied. "But

the action code is *dingo.* If you hear that, all hell is about to break loose."

"Booyah," Wilton said. "Gonna kick some Puke butt today."

"Not unless I give you the code," Chisnall said. "Otherwise, we're just a Puke patrol. Now listen up. No English. Bzadian only. Try not to talk any more than you have to."

"Which dialect?" Monster asked.

"This from the dude who can't even speak English," Wilton said.

"Stick to Corziz," Chisnall said. They all spoke at least three of the alien languages, but Corziz was the most common.

"He's serious, kids," Brogan said. "Anything could trip us up. It might be something about our appearance. Or a word used in the wrong way. It might be the way you blink."

"If anything tips the alien patrol off that we are not what we seem, then the whole Angel program is for nothing," Chisnall said.

They were well trained. That wasn't really what worried him. What worried him was the traitor. Would he or she say or do something to give them up to the patrol? He had to be ready for that. He had to be ready for anything. Without being obvious, he moved up close behind Price.

The far-off plumes of dust grew in size, as did the lingering haze behind them. Two black dots turned into shimmering blobs, then morphed into toy cars, then into Land Rovers. Long-range patrol vehicles (LRPVs), three-seaters. A driver, a passenger, and a gunner position with a fifty-caliber machine gun mounted high behind the two front seats. The rear of the vehicle was a cargo tray.

A few minutes later, the vehicles were close enough for Chisnall to see that they still had their Australian Army markings. The Land Rovers skidded to a halt in the soft dust alongside the Angels, enveloping them for a moment in a mini dust storm.

Showtime, Chisnall thought.

There were no doors on the LRPVs. A tall Bzadian lieutenant swung his legs over the side of the vehicle and stepped down. His uniform had the insignia of the Republican Guards. Chisnall suspected that, judging from his height, he was probably a bobble-head.

There were many races within the Bzadian species. The bobble-heads were one of the more easily identified races because of their unusually tall size (for Bzadians) and their odd habit of nodding while talking.

Chisnall gave Bennett a harsh shove in his back as the lieutenant approached. The SAS man stumbled on his injured leg and fell. *Cruel but effective,* Chisnall thought. Fleming glared at him and helped Bennett back to his feet. The alien lieutenant glanced at the two SAS men and his nostrils flared with distaste.

Chisnall breathed out slowly. This was the moment. The first real test of the whole Angel program. Years in development and years of training, bone remodeling, skin recoloring, learning language and culture. It all came down to this. Could he and his team pass themselves off as Bzadians?

They had tested their disguises in POW camps, but those were artificial environments, and closely monitored. If they had got it wrong, then help was only a few seconds away.

This was the real deal.

The driver of the first Land Rover, a female, got out as well, and they were joined by all three soldiers from the rear vehicle. None of the aliens made any attempt to unholster their weapons, but with the spring-mounted holsters, their weapons would be in their arms in a heartbeat if required. In any case, the machine gunner on the front Land Rover—a young, nervous-looking soldier—had them well covered with the fifty-cal.

The aliens showed interest, Chisnall thought, but no alarm. So far so good.

"You're a long way out," the lieutenant said by way of a greeting, his head bobbing up and down as he talked.

"And glad to see a set of wheels," Chisnall said. "It's a long walk back. I'm Chizna." He raised a clenched fist to his shoulder in what passed for both a salute and a greeting among the enemy soldiers.

"Yozi," the lieutenant said, returning the salute.

"Zabet," Yozi's driver said. Bzadian females—the soldiers at least—usually kept their hair short, but Zabet's hair was long and pulled back in a ponytail. It made her look almost human.

Yozi noticed Chisnall glancing up at the soldier on the fifty-cal and said, "Kezalu, point that thing somewhere else before it goes off."

The young soldier looked a little embarrassed and raised the barrel of the gun to the sky.

"He's new," Yozi said, his head bobbing.

"We all were, once," Chisnall said.

Yozi surprised him by laughing, a short bark. "Hah! Not Alizza." He nodded at one of the soldiers from the second vehicle. "He was born with a coil-gun in each hand."

Alizza grinned, revealing a mouthful of bad teeth, and in the midst of everything, Chisnall found himself wondering why a race with the technology to travel light-years across space couldn't sort out a little dentistry issue.

"Looks like a lot of damage out this way," Yozi said. He scanned the cratered landscape behind them. "The fence is gone."

"Perhaps a rogue missile," Chisnall said. "It did a lot of damage. We were able to walk right through the minefield without problem."

"A rogue missile?" Yozi said, bobbing and shaking his head at the same time. "I can see at least three craters from here. I think it was a deliberate attack on the perimeter."

"It could have been," Chisnall agreed.

Yozi didn't miss a thing. They would have to be especially careful around him.

"Any sign of other scumbugz out there?" Yozi asked. "They must have attacked the perimeter for a reason. Perhaps a ground attack."

"No." Chisnall shook his head. "And if there was a scumbugz army out there, we would have seen it."

"Where did you find these ones?" Yozi asked.

"Just past the hill," Chisnall said. He pointed in the direction they had traveled with a flat hand. Bzadians never pointed with a finger.

"What were you doing out there?" Yozi asked, frowning.

Chisnall said, "Looking for these scumbugz. We were part of a scouting party. But our rotorcraft bugged out in a big hurry just before the air raid."

There was a meaningful glance between Yozi and his driver. Chisnall wondered if he had said something wrong. But his worry was misplaced.

"From Central Field?" Yozi asked.

"Yes," Chisnall replied, hoping that was the right answer.

"You were lucky," Yozi said. "The airfield was hit just after they landed."

"Are they okay?" Chisnall asked. He tried to inject a tone of concern into his voice.

"The rotorcraft took a direct hit," Yozi said. "There was nothing larger than a sierfruit left."

That was a small Bzadian fruit about the size of an egg.

Chisnall looked at him for a moment, then said in a cool voice, "There were friends of mine on that craft."

Yozi covered his face for a moment with both hands, the Bzadian gesture of apology. "Who are the scumbugz?"

"From their uniforms, downed pilots," Chisnall said. "I don't speak human well enough to question them."

"Forward spotters, more likely," Yozi said. "Which

language do you think they speak? Young Kezalu speaks a little human-Chinese."

"I don't know." Chisnall feigned ignorance. "They don't look human-Chinese."

"They all look the same to me," Yozi said. He looked closely at the RAF uniforms. "Their markings are human-English, I think."

Chisnall walked over to Fleming and kicked him viciously in the leg, just pulling back at the last moment so it seemed more violent than it actually was. Fleming clutched at his leg and told Chisnall several very unpleasant things about his mother.

"What do you think?" Chisnall asked. "Sound like human-English?"

"Sounds like animals jabbering to me," Yozi said. "Let's get them back to base. Let the PGZ sort them out."

Chisnall smiled and nodded but felt his guts clench up inside. Since the start of the war, stories had been filtering out of enemy-held territory about the Bzadian secret police, the PGZ. If the stories were true, the PGZ made the Russian KGB look like a support group.

It was said that it was better to die than to fall into the PGZ's hands.

Brogan glanced at him, her expression neutral, but he knew what she was thinking. They were going to deliver two human prisoners to the worst Pukes on the planet. What she didn't know was that they had planned for that possibility.

"What's it like back at the base?" Chisnall asked.

"It's a mess," Yozi said, the grin disappearing instantly. "The scumbugz have hit us hard."

"Everywhere?" Chisnall asked. Implied in the word was concern for his unit. It would be only natural in these circumstances for a soldier to be concerned about his friends and comrades.

"Yes. You're with the Thirty-Fifth," Yozi noted, his eyes flicking over Chisnall's uniform. "I have no news on them apart from the rotorcraft crash."

"As soon as we can, I'd like to return to my battalion HQ," Chisnall said.

"Of course." Yozi regarded him for a moment. *Evaluating him.* "It's a good unit, the Thirty-Fifth," he said.

"We are proud of it," Chisnall said.

"You should be," Yozi said, frowning a little. "What your battalion did in Moscow will make footsteps among the stars."

"Be glad you were not there, my friend," Chisnall said. *Was that the right thing to say?*

"Azoh! The Russian scumbugz would have taken one look at Alizza and given up without a fight," Yozi said.

Alizza grinned fiercely again. He certainly looked like the kind of soldier you would want to have on your side in a battle, bad teeth and all.

The two SAS men were marched to the rear of the first of the patrol vehicles and made to lie on the cargo tray. Chisnall and Brogan climbed up with them, covering the "prisoners" with their sidearms. Wilton, Monster, and Price climbed into the back of the second vehicle. Alizza, after a quiet exchange with Yozi, well out of earshot, climbed onto the rear of the first vehicle, apparently not trusting Chisnall and Brogan to guard the prisoners properly.

Or perhaps to guard Chisnall and Brogan.

Chisnall smiled at him but got only a scowl in return.

Kezalu began to hum to himself as the Land Rovers took off, then to sing, a syncopated reggae-sounding Bzadian song, full of buzzes and clicks. The singing seemed more and more incongruous as they headed toward the pall of smoke in the distance that was the Uluru military base, but Kezalu didn't seem affected by the rising devastation. He began tapping his fingers on the machine-gun mount, keeping his own rhythm. Chisnall caught Yozi's eye and smiled. Yozi rolled his eyes.

Chisnall swapped glances with Brogan as they bumped and bounced across the tussock of the desert floor. He knew they were both thinking the same thing.

If Yozi was convinced, then they had just passed the first test.

If not, then they were about to be hand-delivered to the headquarters of the Bzadian secret police.

Lieutenant Lucky, they called him. He hoped his luck was not about to run out.

8. THE BASE

[0630 hours]

[Perimeter Wall—Uluru Military Base, New Bzadia]

A BOMB-DISPOSAL TEAM WAS WORKING ON AN UNEXploded missile on the outskirts of the base as they approached. It was a German-designed Taurus missile, easily recognizable from the odd, flat-sided shape. It had plowed a hundred-meter-long furrow across the desert before wedging itself up against the low stone wall that marked the perimeter of the military complex.

A bomb-disposal technician was scanning the crumpled shape of the missile with a small device, probably a handheld X-ray machine. Another soldier waved them to a halt, well away from the missile, and directed them onto another road that curved away to their right. It was a road in name only, with stones making two rudimentary lanes through the desert around the perimeter wall.

From inside came the sound of sirens, many of them with different tones, meshed together into a discordant wailing symphony. A hundred separate fires were sending up towers of smoke that merged into a thin, gauzy blanket as they rose. Everywhere were medivac rotorcraft and hospital ships, with their familiar large red crosses on the side—an Earth symbol that the aliens had adopted to avoid confusion.

"That is the third dud I have seen already today," Yozi said, his eyes on the missile as the drivers turned onto the new route.

"Scumbugz technology is junk," Chisnall said, with what he hoped sounded like a sneer. "Lucky for us, eh!"

Yozi twisted around from the front seat of the Land Rover and drilled Chisnall with his blue-black pupils. "There were many more that were not duds. I do not think we were lucky today."

"Of course," Chisnall said. He covered his face with his hands for a moment. After a while he asked, "What do they hope to achieve with a raid like this?"

There was silence. Yozi was still staring at him. Had he seen right through Chisnall's disguise? Chisnall felt naked in front of this creature's dark eyes, as if his human soul were exposed. He willed himself to remain perfectly calm.

"For fifteen years we've been systematically wiping these scumbugz off their own planet," Yozi said. "You think they haven't been watching? Learning? Adapting? They've been studying our tactics, stealing our technology to use against us. Now they're fighting back. If we can't finish them off soon, this planet is going to become a graveyard."

"True," Chisnall said.

He glanced back at the "dud" missile. Yozi was right about the fight back, but he was wrong about the missile. There was nothing faulty about it. There were at least twenty of them scattered over the base, assuming that all of them had got past the alien defenses. Most of the "faulty" missiles were actually radio jammers, sent in specifically to disrupt alien communications. The only working comms in this area right now were those of the Angel Team, operating on a different frequency that was not being jammed.

But not all the duds were radio jammers. Some had a much more sinister purpose.

"Can I use your comm to contact my commander?" Chisnall asked, as if he had just thought of it. "Our comms are not working."

Yozi shook his head. "All radio communication is down."

"How could that be?" Chisnall asked.

"I don't know," Yozi said. "No matter. We will take you to your HQ straight after we drop off the prisoners. Your commander will be very surprised to see you."

"That's for sure," Brogan said.

■ ■ ■

Kezalu continued to sing as they jolted their way around the unsealed track outside the perimeter wall. His voice was a gentle birdsong compared to the harsh wailing that came from inside the base.

Chisnall glanced around and found Alizza staring at him intently. He held his gaze, and eventually Alizza found something else to look at.

Uluru towered over them, dominating the sky. Again and again, Chisnall's eyes were drawn to it. He decided to risk a casual question. "You Republican Guards protect Uluru," he said. "Do you ever go inside?"

Yozi seemed not to have heard the question. "Did you know that human males and females bond for life?" he asked.

"Your ass makes words!" Zabet looked around in disbelief.

"It's true."

"Not always," Brogan said, and added, "I've heard."

"Can you imagine that?" Yozi said. "You take only one mate and stay with them until they die."

"Human lives must be incredibly miserable," Brogan said.

"We will put them all out of their misery," Alizza said.

"Hey, Kezalu." Zabet grinned. "Imagine if you could only be with one female for the rest of your life."

"Might be all right," Kezalu said. "As long as it wasn't you."

"Oh, now you cause me tears," Zabet said, steering the Land Rover around a gaping pothole in the road.

"But think what that must do to the gene pool," Yozi said.

"Each female only has children from one male. No cross-pollination. It's a wonder they evolved at all."

"You call the scumbugz evolved?" Chisnall laughed

"I wonder if humans could breed with Bzadians," Kezalu said.

"That's disgusting," Zabet said.

"You planning to mate with a monkey?" Yozi asked.

"No." Kezalu did not seem at all embarrassed. "Just wondering. Genetically they are almost Bzadian, so maybe in the future we'll be seeing little half-human, half-Bzadian kids running around."

"Not if we wipe them all out first," Alizza said.

Kezalu started singing again.

The singing stopped as the vehicles pulled up to a barrier arm outside a guardhouse. At least ten heavily armed Pukes were standing around, watchful and alert. Chisnall felt all of their eyes upon him, as if any second one of them would spot that he was a fake and raise the alarm.

A young soldier came out of the guardhouse. Yozi held up an ID tube, which the soldier inserted into a hand scanner.

"Do you have a hardline?" Yozi asked. "All comms are down."

The soldier nodded as he handed back the tube. "Get a message to Base Defense, urgent. Tell them the outer perimeter defenses have been attacked. Sector twenty-seven. It could be the forerunner to a ground attack."

"Yes, sir!" The soldier ran back into the guardhouse.

The barrier arm rose and the vehicles started to move.

Into the base.

Right into the heart of the mighty Bzadian war machine.

Chisnall's first impression was that Bzadians were masters of building with rock and stone. He had seen the base many times, studied it in fact from satellite imagery, but it was vastly different seeing it firsthand, and up close.

The scale was almost unbelievable. Buildings, densely packed on wide streets, stretched as far as the eye could see. He knew from the satellite photos that the base covered over a hundred square kilometers of desert, centered around Uluru. But to drive into it was eye-popping. It was an entire city, built in the heart of the desert.

The buildings, often two or three stories high, were constructed of stone blocks. Most were circular or oval in shape. Some were squarish, but with the rounded corners that were a feature of Bzadian architecture.

Many of the buildings were adorned with statues, standing on either side of the entranceway or peering down from the rooftops like gargoyles. They were like nothing he had ever seen before: fierce, jagged-jaw monsters with elongated skulls and deep-set eyes. Chisnall wasn't sure whether these were mythical creatures or actual animals from Bzadia. No human knew what the Bzadians' home planet was like.

Walls were missing off some buildings and roofs off

others. The stone surfaces were inherently strong, and the curved walls allowed pressure waves to flow around them, but even so, he couldn't see a single building that had not been damaged by the missile attack. The head of one of the statues was lying in the middle of the road, staring at them with malevolent stone eyes.

Occasionally, Chisnall would find Kezalu staring down at him from his perch on the fifty-cal. Chisnall was careful to keep his face emotionless and not to show the elation he felt at the hammerlike blow that had been dealt to the aliens' military stronghold.

They passed what appeared to be barracks, mess halls, officers' quarters, and supply stores and armories. Few had escaped unscathed.

Vehicles had been hard hit as well, blown across streets and into buildings by the force of the explosions. Many were still burning fiercely. They passed an airfield that was now just a hole in the ground. The only way Chisnall knew it was an airfield was from the row of rotorcraft jumbled into a pile of twisted metal in the corner. He wondered if this was Central Field.

Ambulances were everywhere, appropriated from Australian hospitals. In some places dead alien soldiers were laid out in long rows.

Fallen rubble and impassable craters closed many of the roads, and it took a long time for the patrol to wind its way through the desolation toward Uluru. They were just turning to back out of a blocked-up thoroughfare when there was a large explosion to the southwest. They all turned to see a cloud of smoke billowing skyward.

"The unexploded missile?" Chisnall asked. The blast had come from that direction.

"I think so," Yozi said. "Perhaps they decided it was safer to detonate it."

"Probably," Chisnall said, knowing that it was much more likely the bomb-disposal team had managed to open the control panel. The booby traps were very well hidden. And very deadly.

The headquarters of the dreaded Bzadian secret police, the PGZ, was to the north of Uluru, in a part of the base that had been relatively unscathed by the attack. The going was no faster here, though, as the roads were full of vehicles, moving in all directions.

They had to pull over to the side at one point and wait for a line of huge alien battle tanks to pass. The tanks had no tracks but moved on four large, ball-shaped wheels. The main gun was a long barrel protruding from a dome-shaped turret at the top. Their heavily armored circular hulls were virtually impregnable. The hulls spun at high speed in battle, and even armor-piercing shells just ricocheted off before they could explode. The earth shook and the Land Rover rattled on its springs as the massive tanks rumbled past.

In a stone city of war, guarded by fierce gargoyles and high-tech weapons, the headquarters of the PGZ still managed to look more menacing than its surroundings. Four stories high, it towered over the one- and two-story buildings around it. There were no gargoyles. It did not need them. Built of a darker stone than the other buildings, it looked like a castle with high, turreted walls. Rooms curved out from the sides of the building. Light burned through narrow oval windows, gleaming like animal eyes in the sparse morning light.

Once again Chisnall felt the cold strangeness. The intuition that had never failed him. This was a bad place. A place of bad things. A place of bad people.

There were no signs of any kind on the building, nor on the tall, jagged wall that surrounded it. Two heavy metal gates provided the only way in or out of the compound. There was no visible security presence, but as their vehicles pulled to a halt outside, a pair of guards emerged from a watch house just inside the gate and waited, weapons in hand, for them to emerge from their vehicles.

"Get the humans ready," Yozi said, and walked over to the gate. He spoke to the guards and after a moment one of them turned and disappeared inside the main entrance to the dark castle.

Chisnall and Brogan covered the two SAS men with their sidearms and motioned for them to get down off the tray of the Land Rover.

Yozi turned back. "ID tubes, everybody." He motioned for them to approach the gate.

Bzadian ID tubes were a matching pair of blue-metal tubes, about the size of a pen, worn on the shoulders like an epaulet. Chisnall unclipped the one from his right shoulder and held it in front of him. The one on his left shoulder he deliberately left alone. It looked exactly like an ID tube but was something else entirely.

The PGZ guard took the tube from him and examined it before inserting it into a scanner unit on his waist. Chisnall waited calmly. The ID was good. Chisnall was sure of that. Human forgers had cracked the Bzadian ID codes months ago, and it was a real ID tube, taken from a Bzadian POW, recoded to Chisnall's profile. There was a moment's pause before it confirmed, with a buzz and a blue light, and the guard handed the tube back to him with three short nods.

The other members of his team and of Yozi's unit all passed their tubes through the gate for checking, taking turns to cover the prisoners as they did so. By the time the guard had finished checking the IDs, the first guard reemerged from the castle, followed by a number of PGZ officers.

It was hard not to cringe a little at the sight of the blood-red uniforms, but a little fear might not look out of place. From what he'd heard, the average Bzadian was more scared of their secret police than humans were.

The gate opened slowly, scraping off to one side, and the guard indicated that Yozi and Chisnall should escort the prisoners inside.

Brogan passed next to him and murmured, "If things get hairy, Fleming is going to try to create a diversion."

Bennett was struggling to stay upright now. The long ride had not done any good to his injured leg. His fierce grimace showed that it was only through sheer determination that he was able to retain his balance as he and Fleming walked ahead of Chisnall and Yozi into the compound. The SAS men were the toughest soldiers Chisnall had ever met, and it was hard not to admire them, but he forced himself to show only contempt for the men.

The smallest of the officers seemed to be in charge. He looked to be quite old, although Bzadian ages were difficult to gauge. He had deep-set eyes like two dark caves and high, protruding cheekbones. His thin, reedy lips were tightly compressed. He stepped ahead of the others and introduced himself with a quick Bzadian salute.

"Goezlin," the PGZ man said, extending the buzzing middle syllable of his name.

"Yozi." He returned the salute.

"Chizna." Chisnall followed suit.

It occurred to him how bizarre it was that a sixteen-year-old human boy with little more than two years' combat training was standing in front of a high-ranked officer in the most feared organization in the enemy army. He forced himself to focus. Everything he said and did here had to be perfect.

"Who captured them?" Goezlin asked.

Yozi indicated Chisnall with a sideways nod.

"Where?"

"Benda Hill," Chisnall said. "Their uniforms are of pilots, but from their location, we suspect they were forward spotters for the raid."

"The outer defenses in that area have been severely

damaged," Yozi said. "It did not look like random missiles. I have alerted Base Defense to prepare for possible infiltrators or maybe a ground attack."

"We were able to pass right through the defensive line near where we captured the humans," Chisnall agreed. "The fence, the guard towers, the minefield—all gone."

Goezlin's eyes peered into Chisnall's, and he wondered if he had said too much.

"What unit are you from?" Goezlin asked, although the answer was clearly marked on Chisnall's uniform.

"Thirty-Fifth Scout Battalion," Chisnall said steadily.

But why had Goezlin asked?

"You're new to the base?" Again the narrow, probing eyes.

"We arrived yesterday, sir," Chisnall said, carefully controlling his breathing.

"And how did you come to capture the humans?"

Chisnall repeated his story of being left behind by the rotorcraft but got only a stony silence. Goezlin suspected something, of that he was sure. But why and what, he could not work out. Their disguises were good. His Bzadian was faultless and his accent perfect. He went back over what he had said. Maybe it was the way he had said it? It couldn't have been anything obvious, or Goezlin would have had them arrested immediately.

Chisnall said and did nothing. Goezlin stared at him.

Without warning, Fleming swung around, sweeping Yozi's feet from under him with an outflung leg. He straightened and cannoned into Chisnall, shoving him into one of the guards. All Chisnall's breath disappeared with a harsh cough and he sprawled backward over the alien.

Fleming was running. Darting toward the narrow opening in the gate. The other guard was there and raising his weapon, but Fleming was too fast and too strong. He grabbed the barrel of the coil-gun as it came up toward him and wrenched it from the guard's grasp. Swinging it around, he knocked the soldier to one side.

Fleming was actually through the gate when the stock of a rifle caught him directly in the face. It must have been like running into a brick wall. He crashed backward.

Brogan kicked the coil-gun out of the dazed Fleming's hands and rested the barrel of her weapon on his forehead as he lay on the ground.

"Good effort, Sergeant," Chisnall said.

Brogan inclined her head slightly but said nothing. She backed away a little and Fleming sat up. He spat out blood.

One of the PGZ guards stepped quickly in and secured Fleming's hands with a metal clasp before he was hauled back in front of Goezlin.

"Get them inside, into the cells," Goezlin said. He smiled, a thin line across his face. "Azoh would be proud, Lieutenant. If all our units were like yours, this war would be over already."

How true that is, Chisnall thought. "Thank you, sir," he said, giving the Bzadian gesture of thanks, his right hand pressed flat to his heart.

Goezlin turned without another word and followed the

two prisoners, now both secured with the metal ties, toward the building.

The gate ground to a close behind Chisnall and Yozi as they returned to the vehicles.

"I will give you a lift back to your unit base," Yozi said. "If there's anything left of it."

Chisnall shook his head. "With the state of the roads, it will be faster for us to walk."

Yozi frowned. "Thirty-Fifth Scout HQ is in the north-western sector. It would take you all day to walk there."

Chisnall was suddenly conscious of Goezlin, still standing on the steps of the building behind them. He shrugged sheepishly. "Of course. I am still a little lost here. This base is huge."

Yozi nodded. "It can be hard to get your head around at first. Mount up. Judging by the amount of damage in that direction, I think we will head out of the base, skirt around the outside, and come back in the northwestern entrance."

"That's good of you," Chisnall said. He pressed his hand to his chest.

As before, Yozi sat up front with Zabet, the driver, while Kezalu manned the fifty-cal. Wilton climbed up with Chisnall and Brogan. The rest of the Angel Team climbed onto the following vehicle.

Brogan shot him a glance as they climbed aboard. The last thing they wanted was to be taken to the headquarters of the 35th Scout Battalion, where they would quickly be recognized as imposters. But it would have seemed odd if he had requested not to go to the headquarters of their unit. And odder still if he had insisted on walking. Somehow they had to part company with Yozi and his team before they got there.

And what about the traitor? What was he or she waiting for before making a move?

9. THE DEAD DRAGON

[0830 hours]

[Exclusion Zone, Uluru Military Base, New Bzadia]

THEY SAW THE CRASH SITE LONG BEFORE THEY GOT TO IT.

It was just a thin tower of smoke in the distance, but with a word from Yozi, they changed course to investigate. The plume of smoke grew thicker, until they could see the crashed aircraft at its foot.

It was a mess. A type three, the one they called the Dragon. A huge and heavily armed jet fighter that made up for its lower speed and lack of maneuverability with an awesome range of weaponry.

Early in the Asian campaign, a single Dragon had taken on a wolf pack of Chinese jet fighters and sent them all crashing into the sea. This Dragon had not been so lucky.

Perhaps it was the sheer weight of numbers of the

attacking human aircraft or just a lucky shot, but the jet had clearly been badly damaged and was trying to make its way back to an airfield in the northeastern quadrant when it had crashed.

Chisnall could imagine the crew nursing the injured fighter back home, realizing too late that the craft was past saving. That sickening feeling as, with the airfield in sight, the heavy airship just gave up and plummeted nose-first into the desert floor.

A plowed-up wave of dirt extended like two pleading arms from where the big plane had come to rest. The nose of the craft was gone, mulched into the dirt by the weight of the plane behind it. The rest of the plane lay broken and twisted, jet fuel leaking from a broken line on one of the wings. Wires and tubing, the intestines of the great creature, spilled out from a jagged rent along one side. The innards were scattered across a hundred meters of desert.

Zabet steered the patrol vehicle around in a sweeping curve and brought them up alongside the plane, just outside the wave carved in the dirt.

"Perhaps a little more distance might be wise," Yozi murmured. Zabet, eyeing the pool of jet fuel a few meters away, quickly complied. They stopped about twenty meters from the plane and dismounted.

Five minutes was all it took to confirm that if the crew had still been on board when the plane had crashed, then they were now part of the desert. They wouldn't have had a chance.

Yozi scanned the desert in the direction from which the big plane had come.

"If they ejected," he said, "they will be out there somewhere."

"What about their personal locators?" Kezalu asked, peering up under the tail section.

"Jammed, like everything else," Yozi said. "We should have a look, in case they are lying out there, injured."

He glanced at Chisnall as if seeking approval, but it was clear that the decision had already been made. They climbed back on board the Land Rovers and started by following the furrow of dirt left by the fuselage of the plane. When that trailed out, they continued on the same compass heading.

Yozi scanned the desert to the left with his binoculars, and Chisnall did the same to his right, although he felt the search was futile. The desert here was dotted with low scrub, and there was little chance of finding anyone. A rotorcraft could cover the same ground in a matter of minutes and would have a far better chance of spotting any pilots, if they had even got out of the plane in time.

He said as much to Yozi as they approached the outer perimeter fence.

Yozi said, "Of course, but it would have been wrong of us not to try."

Chisnall nodded. That was exactly what he would have said, under the same circumstances. He found himself warming to Yozi, despite everything.

Yozi made a circling motion in the air with his finger, and

the Land Rover slowed and turned back on its tracks. Kezalu was humming to himself again. He opened a utility pocket on his uniform and pulled out a slab of bakki, a Bzadian snack that looked like dried beetroot. He noticed Wilton watching, broke off a section, and offered it to him.

"Your soul is warm." Wilton gave the formal Bzadian thank-you and placed his hand correctly over his heart.

"It's a little old and chewy," Kezalu said.

Wilton took a mouthful and grinned. "After a week of combat rations, it'll taste like mother's milk!"

The kid was good, Chisnall thought, using Bzadian slang effortlessly.

They traveled in silence for a while; then Yozi signaled for the vehicles to stop.

Slowly, they pulled to a halt. The dead Dragon was slumped pitifully in front of them, a few hundred meters away.

Yozi scanned the desert to the west.

"You've seen something?" Chisnall asked.

"Was that a movement?" Yozi asked.

Chisnall stared. He could see nothing, just seemingly endless desert and gray-green scrub. Something was wrong. A warning bell clanged inside his head. He turned back quickly to find the snout of Yozi's sidearm pointing directly at his right eye.

The universe seemed to stop moving. A bird above them was cut off midcry, painted onto the backdrop of the sky. Dust particles froze in the air around them, shining in the sun like pinpricks in the skin of the world.

"Azoh!" Chisnall said. "What is this?"

"Who are you?" Yozi asked. When Chisnall did not immediately reply, he added, "Tell your squad to place their weapons on the ground. Now."

"There is no need for this," Chisnall said. "We are soldiers of the Thirty-Fifth Scout Battalion. We—"

"No, you are not," Yozi said. "I don't know who you are, but you are not from the Thirty-Fifth."

"But—"

"You wear the insignia, but not the Moscow Medal. Every soldier in the battalion was given one after the battle for Moscow. They wear it with pride."

Chisnall thought fast. "My squad did not fight in Moscow. We were on—"

"It was a battalion-wide commendation. All members wear it. Except you. Goezlin noticed it too."

So that is what made the PGZ man suspicious.

"You did not know where your headquarters were. Any soldier would have known that from the first hour, let alone the first day. You asked about Uluru. Every soldier is told on their first briefing on arriving on the base never to ask about Uluru."

"We . . ." Chisnall's voice deserted him.

"And just now your man said you had been on combat rations for a week. But the Thirty-Fifth have been on rest leave in Perth since Moscow. They arrived here yesterday. If you've spent a week on rations, then you're not from the Thirty-Fifth. So who are you?"

Chisnall stared at the other soldier. Taking his time. Giving the outward appearance of calm. Any sign of panic or desperation would only make matters worse. In fact, he thought, the best defense might be to go on the offensive. Try to keep Yozi off balance.

An idea occurred to him.

"Very good," he said at last. "Admirable, in fact. You have exceeded our expectations."

Exactly what those expectations were was beyond him at that moment, but he was sure he would think of something.

Yozi frowned and the weapon lowered slightly. "Which unit are you from?"

Which unit are you from? He may have been suspicious, but Yozi still did not consider the possibility that they were humans.

"Obviously not from the Thirty-Fifth." Chisnall allowed himself a smile. "Let me ask you this. Who do you think we are?"

Yozi blinked a few times in quick succession. Clearly, whatever answer he had been expecting, he had not been expecting this. Chisnall leaned back against the sidewall of the vehicle and relaxed, outwardly at least. He tried his best to look like someone who was in charge, not someone who feared for his life.

"Who are you?" Yozi tried again. He sounded less sure of himself now.

Brogan joined in the masquerade. "You tell us."

Yozi lowered the weapon until it was pointing at Chisnall's chest. "You're not PGZ."

"I would have thought that was obvious," Chisnall said, idly allowing his left hand to rest on his belt, on top of one of his frag grenades.

"Fezerker?" Yozi asked. He frowned again.

Above them, Kezalu's mouth dropped open.

Since the start of the war, there had been rumors of an ultrasecret, ultradisciplined alien Special Forces unit. The Fezerkers, operating in secret behind enemy lines.

Whenever something went wrong for the humans—a training accident, a mysterious fire, a faulty missile—it was always thought to be the work of the Fezerkers.

Nobody had ever seen them. No human knew if they really existed.

Until now.

Chisnall stared Yozi straight in the eye and wondered how far he could push this. "Do you know how we recruit new members?" he asked, hoping that there wasn't a recruiting office in every city.

"I only know that you cannot apply," Yozi said.

"You are correct." Chisnall was ad-libbing freely now, and he had worked one of his fingers into the pin of his grenade. "You do not find us. We find you. Understand?" He leaned forward and stared deeply into Yozi's eyes.

Yozi's black eyes widened a little. Chisnall was playing to his ego, making him think he had been noticed.

"We were put next to you to evaluate you in action, without you knowing it. The whole thing was just a setup."

"But the prisoners?"

"We borrowed them from the PGZ. You just returned them for us."

"So Goezlin knew who you were?"

"Of course." Chisnall smiled. "He is an old friend of mine."

Chisnall glanced around. The other patrol vehicle had pulled up about twenty meters away, and Alizza was aiming the fifty-cal right at him.

"You have proof of who you are?" Yozi asked.

"I was wondering when he would ask." Brogan injected a faint note of criticism into her tone.

"Please show it to me," Yozi said.

"You think we should keep it on our uniforms?" Chisnall asked. "Perhaps a flashing sign on our helmets?"

"No, of course not," Yozi said. His gun was now pointing loosely at the floor of the vehicle.

Time to take control, Chisnall thought.

"Your weapon, soldier," he said in a disapproving tone. "It is no longer covering me, but I have not yet proved my identity to you."

"Perhaps our optimism was a little premature," Brogan said.

Yozi looked down at his gun and immediately brought it back up toward Chisnall.

"The proof of your identity," he demanded.

"Better," Chisnall said. "The proof is here."

Chisnall reached down for his backpack and unclipped the top. He started to reach in and glanced at Yozi, raising an eyebrow.

"That's enough," Yozi said. "Pass the pack over here."

"Of course," Chisnall said.

"What is in here?" Yozi asked. He put down his weapon so he could accept the pack from Chisnall.

"A dingo." Chisnall said the code word and dived over the side of the vehicle, the grenade pin in his hand.

Yozi stared in the pack for half a second, registering the grenade inside and the fact that the safety lever was gone.

Chisnall hit the dirt, conscious of Brogan and Wilton a nanosecond behind him. He scrabbled his way through the dirt away from the vehicle, desperate for every inch.

"Grenade!" Yozi yelled. He jumped sideways out of the vehicle. Zabet reacted instantly but Kezalu was slower. He hauled himself up, then seemed to get stuck on something, trapped for a moment in the machine-gun well, his eyes wide with panic. He wrenched himself free, jerked his feet up out of the machine-gun well, and leaped awkwardly from the platform, but it was already too late.

The grenade exploded. The Land Rover seemed to bulge in the middle, inflating like a metal balloon before tearing apart. The explosion was followed immediately by a hollow boom and a ball of flame from the fuel tank.

The heat rushed over Chisnall's head like a blanket,

smothering him. Then it was gone. There was a dull thud in front of him and he opened his eyes to see a jagged shard of metal embedded in the desert an inch from his nose.

Lucky once again.

He was already moving, twisting over and sitting up, even as the flash of heat dissipated around him. His coil-gun whipped out of its back holster into his arms. As fast as he thought he was, he found Brogan already on her feet, her weapon steady on Yozi.

Zabet was lying in a heap near the fiercely burning Land Rover, unmoving. Dazed or dead—there was no way of knowing.

Chisnall turned to the second Land Rover, just in time to see Alizza fly through the air and land face-first on the desert floor while Monster roared and raged like a wild animal behind him. There had clearly been some kind of fight, and it was just as clear who had won. Monster was already climbing up onto the fifty-cal, while Price had the other two Pukes covered with her rifle.

His own weapon sprang into his hands as Chisnall jumped to his feet and ran around to the other side of the vehicle. As he reached its edge, he stopped. There was no need to hurry. Kezalu had been in midair when the grenade had exploded, perhaps half a meter from the Land Rover. He had not stood a chance.

Chisnall walked back around to Zabet and found her dazed and moaning. She was bleeding from the nostrils, but alive. He prodded her with the muzzle of his rifle until she was conscious enough to realize what was happening, then herded her over toward Yozi.

Brogan kept her gun on the two of them while Chisnall walked back to the second Land Rover and disarmed the three soldiers there. Alizza was still spitting out dirt from his headfirst dive into the desert.

A moment later, Yozi's remaining soldiers were sitting in a group, under the watchful eye of Monster on the fifty-cal. Chisnall walked back to where Kezalu lay. His body armor had been shattered by the explosion, and blood was being sucked out of his body by the dry sand of the desert. His eyes were open, though, and his breath was a soft whimper.

His eyes found Chisnall's. They held a quiet question.

Chisnall sat on the dirt next to him and said nothing. Three years of training, but nothing had prepared him for this. This was up close. This was personal. Friend or enemy, it no longer seemed to matter. What was ebbing away in front of him was a life, a living being. He began to hum the soft, sad, syncopated song that Kezalu had sung on the drive. After a moment, the edges of Kezalu's lips twitched up into an almost-smile.

Then he died.

Chisnall called the others over into a huddle, out of earshot.

"We are Oscar Mike in five mikes," he said.

"What are you going to do with the prisoners, LT?" Brogan asked.

A gentle wind murmured around them, bringing with it the smell of the salt lake to the north. The sun had brushed away the cool air of the previous night with a single sweep of morning and sweat began to trickle down the back of Chisnall's neck.

He knew what Brogan was asking. Leaving Yozi and his squad alive would not only compromise the mission, but it might also jeopardize the whole Angel program. If the enemy worked out that humans could disguise themselves as aliens and infiltrate their military bases, they would make security so tight that not even a flea could get in, unless it could prove its off-world ancestry.

"Tie 'em up. Make it secure," he said.

"That's it?" Brogan asked.

Chisnall glanced over at Yozi. "I'm not sure I can kill an unarmed man."

"Not even a Puke?" Price asked.

"I think I could," Wilton said.

"Really, Blake?" Chisnall asked. "Are you really up to cold-bloodedly shooting an unarmed soldier in the face?"

"I think so," Wilton said. "A Puke, anyway."

"And the women?" Chisnall asked.

Wilton's mouth moved a couple of times, but he said nothing.

Chisnall looked around the group. "They don't know who we are. As far as they know, we are a renegade bunch of Pukes. We'll tie them up securely and leave them here.

By the time they are found or work themselves free, we'll be long gone."

"You tie them up out here without food or water and you might as well put a bullet in their heads," Price said. "In fact, that might be kinder. It could be days before they're found."

Chisnall locked eyes with her but said nothing. After a moment she glanced away.

What the desert did to them was the desert's business.

Brogan was staring at him with a strange look in her eye.

"Are we okay?" he asked.

Brogan shrugged, and the others nodded.

They stood, and Chisnall walked over to the group of Bzadian soldiers.

"Why?" Yozi asked.

"That's not important," Chisnall said. He regarded the other soldier for a moment. Two professional warriors, divided by war and one percent of their DNA. In another universe, they might have been friends. "We will tie you and leave you here, and when we get back to base, we will have a rescue party sent out for you."

That last part wasn't true, but it was better to give them hope, Chisnall felt. "Strip off their ID tubes," he said. Even if they somehow got free, they would get nowhere without their ID tubes.

Yozi was shaking his head. "This makes no sense," he said.

It wouldn't, Chisnall thought. As long as Yozi was convinced they were Bzadian, it wouldn't make sense, and that was the way Chisnall wanted it. Better that Yozi think them crazy than realize they were humans.

Yozi looked at the body of young Kezalu, lying nearby. He turned back to Chisnall and his blue-black pupils burned. "It would be better for you if you killed us," Yozi said. "I will come after you."

Chisnall nodded. "I know."

Yozi stared at him for a moment, then held up his hands to be tied.

As soon as they were out of sight, Chisnall held up his hand, and Price, who was driving, pulled over. He took off his helmet and reached inside. He felt around until he found the raised bump that was the secret catch and lifted out the liner. Inside were six packs containing uniform markings. He took out five. Hunter wouldn't need his.

"Replace your insignia with these," he said. "We just changed unit."

The simple image on the patches was recognizable in any language.

"Bomb disposal," Wilton said. "I'm getting a real bad feeling about this."

"There's too much going on around here that I don't know about," Brogan complained as she fixed the patches on her body armor. "If you had been killed back there, none of the rest of us would have had the slightest idea of what to do next."

"Stay tuned," Chisnall said. "You're about to find out. For now, get the fifty-cal down from the top mount and hide it in the back. Bomb techs don't drive around with fifty-caliber machine guns on their top deck."

"One thing I do know is that we're going to be in a huge pile of alien doo-doo if they get loose," Brogan said, glancing back toward where they had left Yozi and his troops.

"True that," Chisnall muttered. Had he done the right thing in leaving them alive?

Almost certainly not.

Perhaps he was not the right person to lead this mission.

10. UXB

[0950 hours]

[Exclusion Zone, Uluru Military Base, New Bzadia]

YOZI WAITED UNTIL THE LAND ROVER DISAPPEARED INTO the blur of the desert. Only when he was sure they were well out of sight did he twist his arms slightly, just once, pulling one hand through the tie and bringing his arms around in front of him.

His bzuntu, his jagged war knife, had not been taken from him, and he quickly used it to cut through the second tie that fastened his ankles.

"Sloppy," Alizza commented, noting the ease with which Yozi had got free.

"Did she look sloppy to you?" Yozi asked as he quickly freed Alizza and the others.

"No." Alizza rubbed some circulation back into his wrists.

His bonds had been tight, to the point of cutting off the blood supply. But Yozi's had been loose. Far too loose. And she had overlooked the bzuntu blade, despite the shaft being clearly visible in the sheath on his inner arm.

Then there was the odd look she had given him as she had tied him: a slight widening of the eyes, nothing more. Or had he merely imagined that?

"Kezalu?" Zabet asked the question nonchalantly, as if it mattered not at all. But it did matter. He could see it in her eyes.

"Leave the body—we can do nothing for him," Yozi said. "We will send someone back for him. Right now we have to get back to Uluru and stop whatever Chizna is up to."

"It's a long way," Alizza said.

"We will head for the crashed Dragon," Yozi said. "There was a lot of wreckage. Azoh may smile on us."

He set out at a run.

Whoever Lieutenant Chizna said he was, he was someone else entirely. When Yozi had met Chizna, he had assumed him to be competent but harmless. That assumption had not done justice to Chizna at all.

[1000 hours]
[Uluru Military Base, New Bzadia]

A soldier directing traffic at an intersection was the first to catch sight of them. He glanced at the insignia on Chisnall's shoulders as they slowed. "This way," he said. He pointed with a flat hand. "What took you so long?"

Chisnall did not reply but caught Brogan's eye as they turned down a road in the direction the soldier had pointed. Immediately ahead of them was the huge four-storied building that was the gateway into the rock. The entrance to Uluru. They were close.

On this side of Uluru, the rock formed massive ridges, like the toes of some gigantic creature. The building was built into a cleft in the rock, a gap between two toes. It was obvious that something serious had happened here, although it was not immediately clear what that was.

The curved front of the building was stone. It looked to be intact. The main way in and out of the building—in and out of Uluru—was by monorail. The track of the monorail, thrust into the air on pillars two stories high, curved in front of them over a parking lot before disappearing into the building through big metal doors. There was no monorail car in sight. On top of the structure, a row of fierce alien gargoyles scowled down at the land around it.

A tall, solid-looking security fence blocked access to the building. Inside the fence was a lot of activity—soldiers running in seemingly random directions. An ambulance was just pulling away through a gate in the fence as they approached. The heavy gate slid quickly shut behind it.

Price gunned the Land Rover forward, past a series of smaller buildings, toward the scene. As they got closer, the reason for the trouble suddenly became clear. The big metal doors where the monorail track entered the building were damaged. There was a gaping hole where the edges of the metal had been bent backward like paper. The doors were warped open, leaving a man-sized gap between the edges.

The Land Rover slowed and stopped at a low outer fence about two hundred meters from the building, where a group of soldiers were manning a barrier arm.

Chisnall leaned out of the window and asked a soldier, "Where's your commanding officer?"

The soldier waved and a tall female came running over.

"What have you got for us?" Chisnall asked.

"Unexploded missile inside the building. It's in the monorail bay, right by the tunnel entrance." She looked nervous.

"Any idea what type?"

"My sergeant thinks it's the one they call 'Tomahawk.'" She struggled with the pronunciation.

Chisnall made himself appear shocked. "A Tomahawk! Why hasn't the area been evacuated?"

"We're doing that as fast as we can. There were some injuries when the missile hit."

Chisnall nodded. "Okay. We'll see what we can do."

The barrier arm lifted and then closed behind them.

"Dude, I don't know squat about disarming a Tomahawk," Wilton said as they accelerated toward the beckoning mouth of Uluru.

"That makes two of us," Brogan said.

"Three," Chisnall said.

▪ ▪ ▪

The security gate slid open as they approached and then closed smoothly behind them. They pulled to a halt at the front entrance of the building and were greeted by a large, square-faced soldier. He looked capable and tough. His uniform markings showed him to be the head of a security detail.

"What the hell was the delay?" he yelled.

"There are unexploded missiles all over the base," Chisnall said. He stepped down from the vehicle and saluted calmly. "I'm Chizna."

"The only missile that matters is this one. It's right by the tunnel entrance," the security officer said. He examined Chisnall for a moment, then returned the salute. "I'm Conna."

"Has the building been cleared?" Chisnall asked.

Conna nodded. "The last of the wounded have just been evacuated."

"Then show us the way," Chisnall said.

Conna led them in through the single door into the building. As they passed into a large entrance room, Chisnall glanced at the door. It was a massive metal contraption with interlocking bars that slotted into the door frame when it was closed.

The entrance room was a blank-walled space, with no exits on the ground level. Conna led them up a flight of stairs against the left wall to a mezzanine level. The balcony of the mezzanine was stone and crenellated like the turret of a castle to provide cover for any defenders while giving them a perfect field of fire down onto the first level.

A single point of entry, Chisnall noted automatically. A single flight of stairs up to an easily defended position. This building was impregnable. The aliens had gone to a lot of trouble to protect what was inside Uluru. Now the tables were going to turn.

From the mezzanine level, a long corridor led deep into the building. A few twists and turns took them past a control room to the monorail bay. A flight of stairs led down from an observation level to the monorail platform. Another flight of stairs led up.

The bay was a mess. One and a half tons of Tomahawk was a lot of energy to disperse, regardless of whether it exploded or not. The missile had smashed through the huge metal outer doors and struck a troop transport car that had been stopped at the monorail platform.

The car had been shunted down and forward by the impact, and the mangled wreckage was now jammed up against a second set of metal doors, behind which lay the entrance to the tunnel. The missile had become embedded in the car. A spiral of smoke or steam was rising from the rear, above the fins. All the lights were out in the monorail bay and the illumination came from outside, sneaking through the rent in the outer metal doors.

"Okay, we'll deal with it from here," Chisnall said to Conna.

"I'll be back shortly," Conna said, looking as though he would rather be anywhere else in the world than in the same space as that unexploded missile.

"You knew this would be here," Brogan said as soon as Conna was gone.

"Of course," Chisnall said.

"How did you know there wouldn't be a real Bzadian bomb squad here already dealing with it?" Price asked.

"Just lucky," Chisnall said.

"Somehow I don't think so," Brogan said.

Chisnall shrugged. "There were unexploded missiles scattered all across the base," he said. "Enough to tie up all of their bomb squads, and then some. This missile was one of the last to arrive, so the real bomb squads would already have been called out to the others."

"Won't a real bomb squad be on their way here soon?" Wilton asked.

"If any of them are left," Chisnall said. "The other duds were all booby-trapped. We were hoping to put as many of the squads out of business as possible before we arrived."

"And how could you guarantee that this missile would make it through the air defenses?" Brogan asked.

"There were three of these. They came in last, after the air defenses had been smashed. The first one to reach the target sent out a self-destruct signal to the others."

"This mission must have been planned for weeks," Brogan said.

"Months," Chisnall said as he climbed down the stairs from the observation level to the monorail bay.

The main doors to the monorail car were a crush of corrugated metal. The windows were all smashed, but the narrow, uneven gaps they left were not big enough to climb through. At the rear of the car there was an emergency door that was still relatively intact, and by clambering up the wreckage, Chisnall was able to get to it. The impact had forced the door from its frame and it jutted open. He wrenched at it, but it was jammed solid. He tried again, with no more success.

"Monster, eat this," he said, which was Bzadian slang for "sort this out."

Chisnall moved out of the way and Monster took his place, wedging his body against a handrail from the observation level that had been bent like a piece of cooked spaghetti. He hauled on the door with both hands. As he strained, whipcord muscles began to stand out in his neck. Nothing happened. He shifted position slightly and tried again. There was a long, slow grinding sound, followed by a terrified shriek from the metal, and the door slowly began to bend, folding back on itself like a tin can being opened.

Within a few minutes the gap was wide enough for them to enter. Monster beat his chest like a gorilla. Chisnall caught his eye and shook his head. It wasn't something a Puke would do.

"Anyway, I loosened it for you," Chisnall said, which earned him a smile.

Monster moved to one side, balancing on the bent railing,

to allow Chisnall access to the car. Chisnall was barely able to squeeze into the narrow gap between the missile body and the crumpled car walls.

The narrow nose of the Tomahawk had entered from the rear of the car, making a fairly neat hole. It was the stubby wings of the missile that had done most of the damage. Rather than slicing through, like the nose, they had snagged and carried the car forward. This left half of the missile—the part in front of the wings—inside the car, while the rest protruded outside. The missile itself was almost undamaged. The front end, which housed the guidance systems, was completely mangled, but the payload, or warhead, section behind that was still in one piece.

Chisnall checked the payload carefully before easing his way back out through the emergency door. He used a mangled piece of the wing to climb on top of the Tomahawk, and sat astride it while he examined the top panels.

"You're sure this won't go off, LT?" Price asked. Her voice was surprisingly steady, considering that if it did explode, there would be only a cloud of vapor where she was now standing.

"Not until we want it to," Chisnall said.

The top part of the aft-body section, just behind the wings, usually contained an extra fuel tank, but that had been removed on this particular missile. Chisnall placed his hand on a panel on the top. There was a pause as it scanned his fingerprints, followed by a click as the panel came loose. He lifted it slightly, then slid it toward the tail.

Monster, still balanced on the railing, looked at him and raised an eyebrow.

Inside was a tightly packed compartment. Chisnall took a quick glance at the contents to check that everything was undamaged.

"Price, get back up to that observation level. Keep an eye out for our square-faced friend." She nodded and disappeared back up the stairs.

Chisnall slid the missile compartment closed.

"What are you waiting for?" Wilton asked. He nodded toward the inner doors of the monorail bay. "This is what we came for, isn't it? Let's get those open and get in there."

"Not yet," Chisnall said.

"Then when?" Brogan asked.

"When the RAF guys get here," Chisnall said.

"Have you forgotten that they're stuck inside the PGZ headquarters?" Brogan asked.

"Not for much longer," Chisnall said.

"Have you got a Get Out of Jail Free card?" Price asked from the platform above.

"Something like that," Chisnall said, smiling up at her. "By the way, they're not RAF. They're SAS."

"Figures," was all Brogan said.

"Here he comes," Price said. "Stand by for company."

"Copy that," Chisnall said. "See if you can find your way up to the roof and get eyes on what's happening back at the fence line. Update me if there is any change out there. Do your phantom thing—don't let anybody see you."

Conna arrived on the upper platform a moment or two later. "Anything to report?" he asked, peering nervously over the handrail.

"We have a problem," Chisnall said.

"What kind of problem?" Conna asked.

"The wiring is all wrong," he said. "This missile has been booby-trapped."

"Can you defuse it?" Conna asked.

"That's what I'm hoping," Chisnall said. He looked at the big metal doors behind the crushed car. "These doors lead straight into the rock—am I correct?"

"Yes."

"You'd better start evacuating whatever is in there."

"That's not possible," Conna said. "So do your job. Make sure it doesn't go off."

"We'll try," Chisnall said. "But it's not that simple. We think the scumbugz are deliberately targeting bomb-disposal teams. We have already lost some good people today."

Conna swore a long violent curse in Bzadian. "What can you do?"

"There is one hope," Chisnall said.

"What?"

"Our comms are down, but do you have a hardline?" Chisnall asked.

"Yes, in the control room."

"Is it still working?"

"So far."

"Good. Contact the PGZ headquarters. I have heard that two human prisoners were taken there a short while ago. Forward spotters for the raid. Find out if this is true. If so, have them brought here," Chisnall said.

"Why?" Conna asked.

"If they were involved in the raid, then they are likely to know about the booby-trapped missiles."

"The PGZ do not like to release prisoners," Conna said.

"Persuade them," Chisnall said.

Conna shook his head, but headed off up the stairs to the control room.

"We'd better act like we're doing something," Chisnall said. He climbed back up onto the wreckage and pretended to examine the Tomahawk.

[1020 hours]

[Exclusion Zone—Uluru Military Base, New Bzadia]

Zabet had found an emergency beacon under a section of the fuselage that had detached and buried itself partway into the desert floor. They had activated it more than half an hour ago. Yozi was starting to wonder if it was functional when a dust plume in the distance announced that help was on its way.

The rescue squad that arrived was surprised and wary when, instead of a downed flight crew, they found themselves approaching a squad of angry Republican Guards.

Yozi hadn't bothered arguing or trying to explain. There was no time for that.

"Take us to PGZ headquarters," he said. When the rescuers seemed unsure, Alizza growled a low noise from deep in his throat, and that was the end of the discussion.

[1050 hours]

[Uluru Military Base, New Bzadia]

Conna came out onto the observation level. "No," he said. "They won't release the prisoners."

"Then persuade them," Chisnall said. "We can't get into the payload to find out what it is, but we are picking up higher than usual levels of radiation. It may be a nuclear warhead."

If Conna had looked nervous before, that doubled now. "Are you sure?"

"No, I'm not," Chisnall said. "Do you want to risk it?"

"Can't they just ask the prisoners? The PGZ can be very persuasive."

"Sure," Chisnall said. "And the only way we will know if the scumbugz are lying is when bits of Uluru start raining down out of the sky. I want those two prisoners standing right next to the missile while we defuse it."

"Uluru is designed to withstand a nuclear attack," Conna said.

"I'm sure that's true," Chisnall said. "But I'm also sure it's not designed to withstand one right at the mouth of the tunnel."

Conna seemed doubtful. "They said there was no way they were—"

Chisnall cut him off. "Look, soldier. I don't know what you've got going on inside that rock, and right now I don't really care. If this missile goes off, then whatever is inside this rock is history. Understand? If I were you, I'd get hold of whoever is in command inside there and let them know that they're about to be vaporized. Then you get them to talk to the PGZ."

Conna disappeared again, and through the window of the control room, they could see him talking animatedly on a handset.

He was back in a few minutes.

"My commander has spoken directly to Commandant Goezlin at the PGZ. The humans are on their way."

"Azoh would be proud, soldier," Chisnall said. "Now, I suggest you put as much distance between yourself and this missile as you can. Tell everyone you can find to evacuate the area immediately."

Conna, for all his fierce looks and tough attitude, took no further convincing. He disappeared with a short salute. Chisnall suspected that when he got to the outer fence line, he was not going to stop running.

"That was almost too easy," Brogan muttered beside him.

Chisnall nodded. "That shows you how important Uluru is to the Pukes. When the Uluru commanders say jump, even the PGZ asks how high."

11. DEFENSE

CHISNALL SLID BACK THE TOP PANEL OF THE MISSILE again and drew out tightly packed bags. The six bags had been wedged together by the impact and he had to separate them before passing them to Brogan, who handed them down to Monster.

"If the PGZ put two and two together, then we may need to defend this place," Chisnall said in English. The time for subterfuge was over.

Beneath where the bags had been was a long aluminum case. He lifted one end and said, "Give us a hand here."

Brogan climbed up alongside him and looked in. She whistled. "You came prepared, LT."

The case ran along the inside of the Tomahawk's body, and they had to maneuver it carefully up through the hatch.

"Got a present for you, Wilton," Chisnall said.

They passed the case down to him. He put it on the ground and flicked catches to reveal a long, black, deadly shape.

Wilton's eyes lit up. "Hello, Momma!"

The M110 SASS 7.62 mm is the standard-issue marksman rifle of the U.S. Army and one of the deadliest sniper rifles in the world. In the right hands, it is accurate up to 800 meters. Wilton had the right hands.

Chisnall and Brogan climbed down.

"Any sign of the SAS guys?" Chisnall asked.

Price's voice came back immediately on the comm. "Nothing yet. No activity at all."

The bags yielded a treasure chest of toys—if your game was to wage a small war.

There were high-explosive C4 packs with timers and remote detonators. Det cord, grenades, standing rockets, and assorted other ways to make loud, dangerous bangs. One pack was full of claymore mines: directional, laser-triggered antipersonnel mines. Very nasty toys.

It also contained a satellite map of the area, which they studied. The building they were in curved into a huge cleft in the cliff face. From the outside it almost looked like a dam. On either side, it was well protected by large spurs of rock that embraced the building. A parking lot was in front of the building and the security fences ran around the entire area. The monorail track ran across the top of it all.

"Brogan, give me an assault plan," Chisnall said. "How would you attack us?"

Brogan studied the map carefully.

"Three-pronged attack—if I had the manpower," she said.

"They do," Chisnall said.

"There are three entry points: the main entrance door, the monorail doors, and the roof entrance. I'd simultaneously blow the main door, rope down a team to the roof from a rotorcraft, and bring a third team up to the monorail doors."

"That's two stories up," Wilton said.

"So they'd hook-and-rope it or just use ladders. They must have fire engines around here. They could bring a couple of those up and use their extension ladders."

"Can we close the monorail doors?" Wilton asked.

"I doubt it," Brogan said. "They're pretty badly buckled."

Chisnall said, "Okay, I want claymores in the monorail bay, just inside the doors. First Puke to step inside will get a heck of a shock, and that should slow down the others."

"We can use standing rockets to take care of any rotorcraft from up here on the roof," Price said.

Standing rockets had proved to be one of the most effective defenses against alien rotorcraft. A development of a weapon the Vietcong had used against American forces in Vietnam, they were a vertical, high-explosive rocket, triggered by the downdraft of a rotorblade.

"Good idea," Chisnall said. "Monster, get the fifty-cal off the Land Rover. Put it somewhere on the roof. Keep it under cover, but make sure you can get into the game real fast."

Monster grunted.

"The Land Rover is parked about here," Wilton said,

pointing to a spot on the map. "Why don't we drop a C4 charge in there, on remote det? Any attack will have to come straight past it."

"Boom!" Monster laughed.

"Good," Chisnall said. "Wilton, take the M110, get up to the roof, relieve Price on top cover."

"Booyah," Wilton said.

"Okay, let's get to it. Price, when Wilton gets there, come down and give Monster a hand getting the fifty-cal out of the Land Rover. Cover it with something so the Pukes will just think we're bringing in some equipment. Drop the C4 charge in while you're doing it. You others, make sure you stay out of sight."

"What are you going to do with the rest of the C4?" Brogan asked.

"I'm going to wire the mouth of the tunnel," he said. "If worse comes to worst, we'll retreat inside the rock and blow the entrance."

"What do you want me to do?" Brogan asked.

"Set up claymores inside the monorail entrance."

"Anything happening, Price?"

"Quiet as Wilton's love life."

"Then let's get into it."

Chisnall went up a flight of stairs to the observation level. From there, a door led into the control room, a small office with large windows overlooking the bay.

He checked a control panel built into a large desk and found the controls for the inner and outer doors. One wall was covered with video screens that showed the building and the area around it from every possible angle. Other screens showed the inside of the building. He could see the members of his team as they got on with their assigned tasks. He watched them carefully for any sign that they were not doing what they were supposed to. But all appeared to be working diligently.

"We should just go in," Wilton complained. He was scouting around the roof of the building for a good shooting position. "Why do we have to wait for the SAS dudes?"

"You're pretty keen to find out what's in there," Brogan said. Chisnall could see her at the end of the monorail bay setting claymores on either side of the big metal doors. She was careful not to be seen through the gap in the doors. She crouched low in a channel that ran down the center of the track.

"Isn't that why we're here?" Wilton asked. "Seriously, LT. Why wait?"

"I already told you what's in there," Price said. She and Monster had wrapped a tarpaulin around the fifty-cal on the back of the Land Rover. "It's a pie factory."

"Whatever it is, Price, it's not a pie factory," Brogan said.

"Well," Price said, "another theory I heard was that they were gene-splicing different species together to create dangerous chimeras."

"What's a chimera?" Wilton asked. His rifle moved slowly left to right, scanning the fence line with its telescopic sights.

"Imagine if a goat and a sheep had a baby. That's a chimera. It'd be a geep," Price said.

"Or a shoat," Brogan said.

"Yeah, well, that's the idea, except goats and sheep can't have babies together, so they do it genetically," Price said. Her breath was shortening as she struggled with her share of the fifty. Monster, who had the heavy end, didn't seem bothered at all.

"The sheep and the goats do it genetically?" Wilton asked.

"No, scientists do, moron," Price said.

"Scientists do it with goats?" Wilton feigned alarm.

"They splice the genes together in test tubes," Price said.

"Doesn't sound dangerous to me," Wilton said.

"What?" Price asked.

"A geep. What would it try and do, baa you to death?" Wilton said.

"That was just an example, moron," Price said. "What if they crossed snakes and birds and produced birds with fangs and deadly venom?"

"They already did. It's called Sergeant Brogan," Wilton said.

"Venomous birds would be kinda scary," Chisnall said.

"How about elephants and kangaroos?" Monster said. "If they crossed those."

"That wouldn't be scary, just funny," Chisnall said.

"Not if one landed on top of you, my dude," Monster said.

[1110 hours]

[PGZ Headquarters, Uluru Military Base, New Bzadia]

"Get Goezlin, now!" Yozi roared through the gate at a PGZ guard.

"Where are your ID tubes?" the guard asked.

"Azoh! I don't have them, and if you don't get Goezlin down here now, you'll be fishing yours out of your ear."

There was movement near the entrance, and the problem was solved by the appearance of Goezlin. He must have been watching the scene through a window or on a security monitor.

"Lieutenant Yozi," Goezlin said. He made no movement to have the gate opened.

"Yes, sir. The prisoners we brought you earlier, sir. Where are they now?"

Goezlin did not look happy. "They are no longer here. They were required elsewhere."

"Sir, I have reason to believe that they are not who they seemed. My team and I were attacked by the squad that brought them in. There is something very strange going on here."

"They attacked you?"

"And killed my machine gunner. Where are the scumbugz now, sir?"

Goezlin's eyes narrowed even farther, if that was possible. "They have been taken to help defuse an unexploded missile."

"Where?"

"At the entrance to Uluru."

■ ■ ■

Price came to help Chisnall set the C4 charges on the top story of the building, at the very rear, where the building met the cliff face. He created a shaped charge by stacking six C4 packs in a three-two-one pattern.

"Rock looks pretty solid," Price said.

"That's been worrying me a little," Chisnall said. "If we could drill into it, I'd be happier. But at the very least these charges should bring the building down. Hopefully create enough rubble to block up the entrance. Buy us some time. Everything else look okay?"

He felt like he was asking her about her end-of-year exams instead of their plans to defend a building from alien attack.

"All good," she said.

"Movement at the fence line," Wilton reported from the roof.

"Looks like it could be the PGZ guys with Fleming and Bennett."

"Okay," Chisnall said. "Showtime. Price, get on the roof with the others and load your grenade launcher with smoke. Don't be seen. Brogan, I want you down by the front door. I'll coordinate from the control room. Nobody does anything except on my go."

There was an altercation at the fence line. Chisnall watched it on one of the security monitors. The guard was arguing with two red-suited PGZ officers.

It didn't last long. Nobody argued with the PGZ.

They got back in their vehicle and the barrier arm lifted to allow them through. The car rolled forward slowly, then accelerated.

"Wilton, give me a range on that vehicle," Chisnall said.

"Three hundred and twenty meters. And closing," Wilton said from the roof.

"Keep coming," Chisnall said under his breath.

"Two hundred and eighty meters," Wilton said.

"All units check in," Chisnall said.

"Angel Two in position," Brogan said.

"Angel Four in position."

"Angel Five in position."

"Angel Six in position."

For a moment Chisnall found himself waiting for one more voice. But Angel Three was not going to check in. Not now. Not ever. With the odds stacked against them, they could have used Hunter on their side. More than that, Chisnall could have used a friend's shoulder to lean on.

"Two hundred meters," Wilton said.

Once the SAS guys were inside, the Angel Team should be able to hold their defensive perimeter long enough for the two men to do what they needed to do, Chisnall thought. But if the PGZ figured out what was really going on, then it was all going to get messy really fast.

It got really messy really fast.

"One hundred and eighty meters," Wilton said. "LT, I got eyes on a vehicle advancing at speed down the southern approach road."

Chisnall repositioned one of the cameras to see what Wilton was looking at. A Land Rover with two soldiers in the front seats and a bunch more on the tray.

"This is about to turn pear-shaped," he said. "Stay frosty. What's the range to the PGZ car?"

"One hundred and forty meters."

"Not close enough," Chisnall said. "Price, on my mark, lay some smoke. Two canisters."

"One hundred and thirty meters."

The Land Rover was sliding to a halt at the barriers. There was shouting and waving. The PGZ car, well over halfway toward them, slowed, then began to turn back.

"Wilton, take out the tires on that PGZ car!" Chisnall yelled.

There was a crack from overhead and the left front tire disintegrated, sending black pieces of rubber flying. The car slewed off the road and ground to a halt in the dirt.

Almost immediately, the back doors opened and Fleming emerged, dragging Bennett with him. The front door of the car began to open. Fleming kicked at it, slamming it shut. They began to run toward the building.

"Suppressing fire!" Chisnall yelled, and heard the fifty-cal open up overhead. Dust kicked up around the PGZ car and the bulletproof windows shattered.

The PGZ officers scrambled from the vehicle, taking cover behind it.

"One hundred and twenty meters," Wilton said.

"Smoke, smoke, smoke!" Chisnall yelled.

A second later, a spinning canister came into view, followed quickly by a second. The canisters landed behind Fleming and Bennett and spewed out white smoke, almost instantly creating a dense fog. The soldiers, the fence line, and even the buildings behind them faded into vague silhouettes, then to nothing.

They were getting incoming fire now; he could hear the rounds hitting the building around them. The Pukes were firing blind, but Fleming and Bennett were taking no chances, running a zigzagging course toward the building so as not to present an easy target. Surely they were no more than a hundred meters now, thought Chisnall.

Monster's fire from the roof of the building was constant. He, too, was firing blindly into the smoke. Anyone in their right minds would have hit the deck and stayed there. Wilton, also on the roof, was peppering the PGZ car, keeping the two officers cowering behind it.

The smoke swirled and parted near the fence line and the nose of the second Land Rover raced through it at speed, the fifty-cal on the back firing continuously. Fleming heard it and pushed Bennett to the ground as bullets kicked up dust around them. The faces of the enemy soldiers were clearly visible on Chisnall's screen.

"It's Yozi! Price, switch to frags!" Chisnall yelled.

"Copy that," Price said.

A few seconds later he heard an explosion and saw a volcano of dirt erupt in front of the Land Rover. It lurched to the side but kept coming. Another grenade, another explosion, this one just in front of the Land Rover. It bucked and jumped, flipping onto its side.

Fleming pulled Bennett back to his feet and hauled him toward the building at the base of Uluru.

Fifty meters, twenty, ten, then the fifty-cal on the Land Rover opened up again. The big Puke, Alizza, had wrenched it off its mount and balanced it on top of the overturned vehicle.

"Get them inside!" Chisnall yelled.

On one of the monitors, he saw the front door of the building open, just as the SAS men reached it. Puffs of rock dust kicked out of the side of the building around them and sparks flew from the heavy metal door. He could see Brogan putting her weight behind the door, starting to close it as Fleming and Bennett ran inside.

More sparks from the door, hammer blows of the heavy machine-gun rounds, then suddenly Brogan was gone. Her head snapped back and her body fell away out of sight. There was a momentary gasp on her comm, then silence.

"Brogan!" Chisnall yelled. There was no reply. "Brogan!"

"They're pulling back," Wilton yelled from the roof. "Booyah!"

"I think Brogan's down," Chisnall said. He left the control room and ran toward the entrance.

The corridors seemed endless. They felt unreal, like a movie set. He had been able to deal with Hunter's death, but that had been different. Hunter had been dead when they had found him. Chisnall hadn't had to see him go down, like he had seen Brogan go down. Her head snapping backward with the impact of a bullet. Her limp, lifeless body falling.

He reached the mezzanine floor and saw Brogan lying behind the door. The door was shut, and Fleming was closing the interlocking bars around the perimeter to keep it that way.

Bennett was leaning over her. He looked up as Chisnall entered.

"Is she . . . ?" Chisnall found the words got stuck in his throat.

"She's alive but out cold," Bennett said. "Took a bullet to the helmet. Helmet shattered and absorbed most of the force. I think the real damage happened when her head hit the floor."

The ground seemed unsteady, and Chisnall grabbed at the railing of the mezzanine wall for support.

Then he keyed his comm. "Brogan's down, unconscious. Everybody relocate to the entrance. It won't take them long to call in reinforcements."

He ran down the stairs and kneeled beside Brogan. Her shattered helmet lay beside her head. Blood flowed from a cut somewhere in her hairline, but it didn't look serious. Her eyes were shut and she was breathing steadily.

"That was a little tight," Fleming said.

"The timing was a lot closer than we expected," Chisnall said without looking up.

"How did they get onto us so fast?" Bennett asked.

Chisnall glanced at him. There was no choice but to be honest.

"My fault. Sorry," he said. "You remember Yozi and his team, who picked us up in the desert?"

"Yes," Fleming said.

"We left them out there. Alive. I just couldn't bring myself to execute them in cold blood."

Fleming and Bennett looked at each other but said nothing.

"How long do you need to remove the warhead?" Chisnall asked.

"Ten to fifteen mikes," Bennett said. "If all goes well."

"You're removing the warhead?" Price asked, arriving on the mezzanine level.

"You haven't told your team yet?" Bennett asked.

"My orders were not to, until we were actually inside the rock," Chisnall said.

"Maybe it's time," Fleming said.

12. THE ATTACK

[1200 hours]
[Uluru Secure Facility, New Bzadia]

CHISNALL STARED AT THE BANK OF SCREENS THAT COVered the wall of the control room. Cameras covered every angle outside the building. Some showed the surrounding area and the fence lines. Others, presumably mounted in the monorail track, showed the view back toward the building they were in.

This place was a fortress, but no fortress could withstand what the aliens were about to throw at them for long.

Brogan lay in the middle of the room. She had not yet regained consciousness. That worried him more than he liked to admit. Was she just unconscious, or comatose?

He said, "It's time you knew why we are here."

"No argument from me," Price said.

Chisnall nodded. "I wanted to tell you earlier, but my orders were for total secrecy."

"So what's it all about, dude?" Wilton asked. "What's really, like, going on inside this rock?"

"That we don't know. But with all the secrecy and security surrounding it, you don't have to be a genius to work out that it's vital to the Pukes. And if it's that important to them, then it's probably just as important for us to stop it. But how? Uluru is so big, and so solid, that we knew we couldn't touch it, not even with a nuclear attack. So we crash-landed the Tomahawk here, right at the entrance. It's a CL-22 warhead."

Wilton whistled. "China Lake Two Two. Powerful stuff."

CL-22 was the latest derivative of the immensely powerful CL-20 explosive invented back in the twentieth century. CL-20 had been developed as a propellant, but CL-22 was created for use in nuclear warheads. It was the most powerful conventional explosive on Earth.

"I thought our mission was to find out what's going on inside the rock," Price said.

"Partly," Chisnall said. "But the other part is to get Fleming, Bennett, and that warhead inside the rock so they can destroy it. Whatever it is."

"This is starting to sound like a suicide mission," Wilton said.

"Only if we're still here when the warhead goes off," Chisnall said. "And I'm not planning on hanging around for that party."

"The Monster hope you have other way out," Monster

said, "because the Monster doesn't think we're coming back this way."

"There's another exit from this tunnel," Chisnall said. "The monorail track runs right through the rock and comes out the other side. But we've never seen them use it. We think it's an emergency exit. According to our satellite imagery and ground-penetrating radar, it is blocked by two, maybe three sets of blast doors."

"And you're betting our lives on this?" Price said.

"Pretty much," Chisnall said. "But it's a good bet. The monorail runs from there out into the desert, to some kind of safety bunker. That's our extraction point."

"Sounds pretty hairy to me," Wilton said.

"Did you sign up for the easy mission, Wilton?" Price said. "Sorry, that's next week."

"Right now we need to make sure we can hold off the Pukes long enough for Fleming and Bennett to extract the warhead," Chisnall said.

"What's taking them so long?" Wilton asked.

It had already been ten minutes since they had shown them where the missile lay entangled with the monorail car.

Chisnall keyed his comm. "Fleming, sit rep, over?"

Fleming came back immediately. "It's slow going. The way the car crushed around the nose of the missile has made extraction difficult."

"Anything we can do to help?" Chisnall asked.

"No. We're working through it. What are our friends up to?"

Chisnall ran his eyes over the bank of monitors one more time. The area was still clear, although the Bzadians had occupied all the surrounding buildings.

"All quiet on the eastern front," Chisnall said.

"What's keeping them?" Price asked.

"They're preparing for the assault," Chisnall said.

"We've got movement," Monster said, pointing to one of the monitors.

Chisnall stared. Something was crawling past a gap between two of the buildings. Something big. It emerged onto the roadway by the side of the building and stopped. A moment later it was joined by a twin.

"Holy crap," Wilton said.

The two huge alien battle tanks barely fit on the roadway. They skulked in the shadows between the buildings, unstoppable, ironclad juggernauts.

"They'll use them as cover," Chisnall said. "Bring up the infantry behind them, then blow the front door."

"What can we do?" Price asked.

"Nothing," Chisnall said. "We are not going to engage anyone until they are inside the building. The doorway will create a bottleneck, so we don't have to engage the entire force at once. Fleming, Bennett, we're expecting company. How long do you need?"

"Could be a half hour, not sure."

"What happened to ten mikes? I don't think we have thirty," Chisnall said.

"We'll do our best," Fleming said.

Chisnall picked up the remote detonator, a small black device like a remote control, with a numeric keypad and a fire button. It could be coded to any number of different explosive devices and was currently keyed to the C4 charge in the Land Rover outside. He checked the safety was on and placed the detonator carefully on the desk, next to the controls for the monorail bay doors.

Seconds ticked by, turning into minutes.

The Bzadian forces remained in position.

He picked up the detonator, checked it again, and put it back down.

Sweat trickled slowly down the back of his neck. His breathing seemed unnaturally loud in the silence.

"What are they waiting for?" he wondered out loud.

"Come on already," Wilton said. "Bring it on."

"You in a hurry to die?" Monster asked.

"No, you?" Wilton asked.

"You need a nervous system to feel scared, and I don't think Monster has one," Chisnall said.

"LT!" It was Price.

Chisnall looked back at the screen showing the area in front of the building.

A monorail car had appeared around the corner of the track. It slowed and then stopped near the battle tanks.

"There's something strange about that car," Chisnall said. He used the controls on the desk in front of him to zoom in.

"They've welded something to the front of it," Wilton said.

It was a heavy metal wedge.

"They're going to ram the front doors!" Chisnall said.

That would bring them right into the monorail bay, where Fleming and Bennett were working.

"Any C4 left?" Price asked. "We could blow the track."

"A couple of packs. But I don't think we've got time, and anyone who goes out there will be a leaky sieve in a matter of seconds," Chisnall said.

"I can do it, skipper," Price said.

"No way, Phantom. Not even you can get out there without being seen," Chisnall said.

"Think I can, skipper," Price said. "That channel in the center of the track. I should be able to worm my way along it. I'll stash a pack of C4 just past the first pylon."

"They could attack any minute," Chisnall said.

"Then let's not fart around anymore," Price said.

"Okay. Remember to disable the claymores first," Chisnall said.

"You think?" Price said.

Chisnall handed her the pack, and she disappeared. A moment later she appeared on one of the monitors, inside the monorail bay.

"Be quick," Chisnall said. "Everybody else, get to your positions."

He glanced down at Brogan, who was still unconscious on the floor of the control center. She was breathing steadily and there was no time to worry about her now.

Monster and Wilton headed off toward the entrance.

Price moved out of view and Chisnall watched one of the screens that looked down on the monorail track. The C4 pack appeared first, sliding along a shallow channel in the track as if under its own steam. Then an arm came into view, followed by Price herself. She wormed her way along the channel, wriggling like a snake, never lifting herself up a hair more than she had to.

Price was still his most likely suspect. She was the only person he knew who could have infiltrated the hangar and tampered with the half-pipe. But it was hard to reconcile the idea of Price the traitor with the bravery and determination he was seeing on the monitor. If she was a traitor, why would she be putting herself at such risk to help the mission succeed?

The same could be said for any member of the team, he realized.

Chisnall kept one eye on the other screens. There was a lot of activity over between the buildings, but so far the tanks, the car, and the troops were remaining in position. Price was about halfway to the pylon now.

The two behemoths—the Bzadian battle tanks—began to move.

"Price, hurry it up," Chisnall said. "They're moving. Everybody else, ready, ready, ready."

He pulled his visor down into combat position.

The monorail car stayed where it was. That made sense. It would wait for the tanks to close in on the building before speeding into the attack. He couldn't see it, but he could guess that the car was full of heavily armed soldiers. If it got inside the bay, then it was all over. All their defenses depended on only a few soldiers making it through the main entrance at one time.

There was movement in the sky to the south, and three rotorcraft flew into view on one of the monitors. From the shapes of the craft, they were a couple of troop carriers and a gunship. That explained the delay while they prepared their attack. The tanks were speeding up now, rumbling over the crossroads and over the low outer fence as if it didn't exist. At least two full squads of infantry ran behind them.

"Keep out of the entrance until they blow the door," he said. "I think they're going to hit it with a tank shell."

Monster and Wilton were on the mezzanine level, well away from the blast area, but the force of the explosion could still be deadly in that confined space.

"Copy that," Wilton said.

On the monorail track, Price had reached the pylon. She wriggled forward another two meters and pushed the C4 pack out in front of her as far as she could.

She began to wriggle backward but it was painfully slow going.

"Too slow, Price," Chisnall said. "You're going to have to turn around."

"If I do that, skipper, they'll see me."

"There are incoming rotorcraft; they're going to see you in a few seconds anyway."

He keyed the code for the C4 pack into the detonator but

left the safety on. If she didn't get back inside the monorail bay, she was going to be toast.

Price quickly pushed herself up onto her hands and knees, twisted over, and lay back down in the channel, wriggling forward as fast as she could. Even that single glimpse of her was enough for the aliens. Rounds cracked into the monorail track around her.

She had made it less than a meter away from the pylon when the monorail car began to move. The tanks were halfway across the security zone now, bearing down on the inner fence. They were heading straight for the main door of the building.

"The car is moving!" Chisnall yelled. "Price, get out of there."

He flicked the safety off on the detonator.

Price jumped to her feet and began to run. Rounds split the air around her and puffs of white flicked up around her feet. The car was only meters behind her, closing down on the last pillar. Chisnall's thumb moved over the firing button.

"Fleming! Bennett! Get down!" he yelled. Even inside the monorail bay, the shock wave of the blast would be teeth-rattling.

There was an explosion below him and the building shook as the tanks fired at the main door. He took one more look at the slender figure of Price, the Kiwi Phantom. She was bent over, legs pumping as she sprinted along the track toward the big metal doors of the monorail bay.

"Blow it!" Wilton yelled. "You gotta blow it!"

Just a couple more seconds and she'd be safe. But Wilton was right. He didn't have a couple more seconds. Price didn't have a couple more seconds.

She dived.

He pressed the firing button.

There was a half breath while the detonator translated the instruction from the trigger; then a brilliant flare whitened out the screen he was watching. It cleared as the whole building shook from the blast. The window looking down on the bay shattered, and glass exploded into the room around him, clattering off his body armor and visor. Several of the monitors blanked out as the blast took out their cameras.

He had instinctively ducked down, and now he straightened, his eyes glued to the screens.

The monorail car was in midair, the metal wedge at the front aimed skyward like the nose of a rocket ship. In slow motion, it started to fall backward. It struck the remains of the rail and tumbled over as it crashed into the ground below.

Amazingly, he still had a view back toward the building. A camera on the monorail track, on one of the outer pylons, had survived. He could see the gaping hole in the monorail line and still had a view of the doors to the monorail bay. Big, heavy, and jammed by the impact of the Tomahawk, they had barely moved.

"Price? Price?"

There was silence.

"Price!"

He ran to the smashed window and looked down into the monorail bay. Would he see a body, or would there not even be that much of her to find? The bay was full of smoke and dust from the explosion. It took him a moment to find her. She wasn't dead. Far from it. She was sitting on the floor of the bay, below the heavy rail. She grinned up at him and gave him a thumbs-up.

Chisnall shook his head in amazement and gave her a thumbs-up back. Nobody but Price could have pulled off that stunt. She must have slipped through the opening to the bay in the microsecond before the blast and dropped down to the safety of the bay's floor.

He quickly checked on Brogan, who was okay but still unconscious. She had been shielded from the flying glass by the control desk. He spotted Price walking past the control room, heading for the entrance.

"Incoming tanks and rotorcraft!" Wilton yelled.

Chisnall raced back to the screens.

The tanks were rolling up toward the hole their guns had just blasted where the main door used to be, still providing cover for the infantry crowded behind it.

Chisnall could see two rotorcraft above them racing toward the roof of the building. Soldiers with their weapons ready crouched on the slipways over the rotorblades. The gunship held back. He forced his eyes away from the rotorcraft. The standing rockets on the roof should take care of them. Wilton had deployed four in a line across the front of the rooftop, just behind the parapet wall.

One of the tanks was rolling right toward the Land Rover parked outside the building, regarding it as merely an annoyance to be barged out of the way or crushed.

The troops were crouching and running along behind the two tanks. Ten meters to go before the tank hit the Land Rover. Chisnall keyed the second code into the detonator and rested his thumb lightly on the trigger. Around him, the building began to vibrate and the images on the screens quivered to the low bass rumble of the tank wheels on the rocky ground.

One of the rotorcraft moved over the roofline of the building, the other not far behind it. There was a flash on one of the monitors and a loud bang overhead as one of the standing rockets was triggered.

He saw the rotorcraft spin wildly out of control, falling. Soldiers flew off like a cloud of insects. The craft hit the edge of the roof and upended. For a second he was looking down on the spinning, fractured blades of the rotorcraft as it fell. It slipped sideways and struck the red rock of Uluru before hitting the ground and exploding.

Below, the big ball wheels of the Bzadian battle tank rolled over the top of the Land Rover, crushing it, flattening it.

Chisnall pressed the trigger.

There was a huge roar and a brilliant flare. The desert itself seemed to be swallowed by the explosion as dirt and dust mushroomed out around the big metal creature. The edge of the tank lifted into the air impossibly slowly. Just when

Chisnall thought it would settle back down, it continued to rise, past its center of gravity, then over, while its wheels continued to grind like the legs of a nearly dead beetle.

The dust began to clear and there was no sign of the infantry. It was as if they had vanished into thin air. Then the floor of the desert began to shiver, and Chisnall realized that he was seeing the dust-covered shapes of soldiers rising up out of the desert and beginning to retreat.

The second tank began to back away, wary that the same fate lay in store for it.

"Get that fifty-cal ready, and stay frosty," Chisnall said to Monster. Already he could see a second wave of infantry charging over the ground toward them. And the second rotorcraft was keeping well away from the roofline.

"How's that warhead coming?" Chisnall asked as he keyed the third code into the detonator. The code for the massed charge above their heads. He made sure the safety was on. This charge would take down the whole building—at the very least.

"About five mikes," Bennett said. "We've extracted it—prepping it for transport now."

Chisnall clipped the detonator to his belt and ran out of the control room with just one backward glance at the prone form of Brogan. She would be as safe here as anywhere. Everything now depended on them holding off the enemy until the SAS guys finished whatever it was they were doing.

His coil-gun sprang into his hands as he raced down the long, featureless corridor toward the entrance. He ran out onto the mezzanine. Monster had the fifty-cal propped up at the top of the stairs. He grinned at Chisnall, ready for a fight.

Wilton stood at the other end of the mezzanine, his sniper rifle resting on one of the gaps in the thick stone wall. Price was on the ground floor laying claymores among the rubble of the demolished doorway.

"Get out of there," Chisnall yelled.

"Almost done," Price said.

Chisnall took position behind the wall and trained his gun on the doorway as Price skipped lightly up the stairs, stopping to arm another couple of claymores that she had wired to the underside of the metal staircase.

She took position behind the wall of the mezzanine.

From outside they could hear the sound of running boot steps.

"Hold your fire," Chisnall said. "Let the claymores deal with the leaders."

The sound of the boots was louder now. Then suddenly it stopped. No soldiers were in sight.

"Prepare for flash-bangs!" Chisnall cried.

He dropped down behind the safety of the balcony wall. Next to him he saw Monster screw his eyes tightly shut and clamp his hands over his ears. There were thuds from below them and he tensed, waiting for the explosions. They came with a wave and a roar of light, heat, and dust. He spun back around, raising his rifle to his shoulder.

"Hold your fire!" he yelled.

Three alien soldiers rushed into the entranceway, rifles at the ready. The claymores triggered on either side, and the three disappeared in a hailstorm of smoke and dust, thrown backward by the shock wave. It probably hadn't penetrated their suits, but it would stun them for a while.

"Suppressing fire!" he yelled.

He let loose a long burst at the ragged hole where the door used to be. The others joined in. They were firing at shadows, but the doorway was now a death trap. No soldier would willingly run into such a maelstrom. Instead, the Pukes tried attacking from the sides, holding their weapons around the broken corners of the walls and firing blindly up at the mezzanine.

Chisnall pulled a frag grenade off his belt, set the timer for one second, pulled the pin, and threw it.

"Frag out!" he yelled.

The grenade hit the ground just outside the doorway and exploded. The firing from either side stopped. Chisnall's ears rang from the thunder of the weapons inside the stone walls, a high-pitched whistle inside his head.

"Everybody okay?"

He got a chorus of "Oscar Kilos" in return.

"What now, LT?" Price asked.

"Hold fast," Chisnall said. "Stay frosty, they can't—" He stopped, listening. Below them, on the floor of the entranceway, the dust was alive. The rubble was quivering, and from outside he could hear an unmistakable rumbling.

"Tank!" he yelled. "Relocate now!"

They were too late. The outer wall of the building disintegrated with a roar, and the pressure wave knocked him backward. When Chisnall regained his feet, he saw Price and Wilton lying in the dust. Monster was just clawing himself back upright. The tank was outside, clearly visible through the broken front of the building. It rolled right up to the hole made by the explosion.

And the barrel of its gun was rising toward the mezzanine.

13. THE TUNNEL

"MOVE!" CHISNALL YELLED. "MOVE!" HE GOT ONLY GROGGY stirrings from his team.

The round shape of the battle tank blocked all the light, turning the day into twilight. The barrel of the gun rotated as it rose toward him. He tried to will his legs to walk, to run. But there was no time.

The fifty-cal began to fire. Through the swirling clouds of dust, Chisnall saw Monster, sighting down the barrel, emptying his magazine at the Bzadian battle tank. An act of desperation. Machine-gun rounds would have no effect on a tank.

It all seemed to be in slow motion: the rising of the tank's gun barrel, the fire from the fifty-cal, the sparks from the end of the barrel as the rounds impacted. Now Chisnall realized what Monster was doing: He was pouring his fire right down into the barrel. Huge fifty-cal machine-gun bullets were spitting directly into the small black circle that was the mouth of the gun.

There was a loud crack from the tank and the barrel of the tank's gun bulged and then split as the shell detonated inside it. Fractured pieces of metal flew out into the air.

"Good effort, Monster!" Chisnall yelled in excitement and relief.

"Cheese and rice!" Monster said, looking more surprised than anyone.

The tank began to back away, its main armament destroyed. Then it lurched to a halt, dead in the water.

Wilton and Price were on their feet now, looking dazed.

"Are you okay?" Chisnall asked.

Price shook off dust like a dog shaking off water. "Just winded," she gasped.

Wilton gave him the thumbs-up.

"Let's move," Chisnall said. "Relocate to the far end of the corridor."

Chisnall slung his rifle and went to pick up one end of the fifty-cal. Monster grabbed his hands before Chisnall could touch it, spitting on the barrel as he did so. The spit sizzled and evaporated instantly.

Idiot! Chisnall thought. Burned hands were all he needed right now. He should have known that the barrel of the gun would be red-hot. Monster handed him a thick cloth and he wrapped it around the barrel.

Boot steps sounded in the shattered entranceway and enemy rounds sprayed up into the ceiling of the corridor as they ran. They set the fifty-cal on the floor at the end of the corridor and Monster lay behind it. Wilton kneeled at the doorway, his rifle propped on his knee. Price and Chisnall took opposite sides of the doorway. Anyone foolish enough to stick his head around the other end of that corridor was going to lose it, real fast.

They waited. They could hear sounds coming from the other end of the long corridor, but there was no sign of anyone.

"The tank shell took out the stairs," Price said. "They'll have to bring up some ladders."

"That won't take long," Chisnall said.

"We're done." It was Fleming's voice on the comm. "We're Oscar Mike."

Finally!

"Monster, stay here," Chisnall said. "Keep their heads down. Price, Wilton, on me. I'm going to open up the doors to the tunnel."

They ran for the control room with the others and had just reached it when he heard the heavy stutter of Monster's fifty-cal in the corridor behind him.

Brogan was sitting up but looked dazed.

"Brogan!" Chisnall tried to keep the relief out of his voice. "Are you okay?"

"I . . . I think so," she said. She seemed vacant.

"Can you walk?"

"I don't know." Her voice came from somewhere far away.

Chisnall hoped it was just the aftereffects of the concussion and not something more permanent.

"Price, Wilton, take her with you. Get her inside the tunnel when I open the doors."

He found the controls for the inner bay doors and shoved them open. Through a long glass window that looked out on the monorail bay, he could see the two SAS men already in the bay and waiting. Behind the wreckage of the car and the Tomahawk, the doors began to open.

Price and Wilton appeared on the stairs, Brogan stumbling between them.

"Grenades!" Monster yelled from the passageway.

"Get out of there!" Chisnall yelled.

"Monster did this already," Monster said, running at full speed past the door to the control room.

The grenades in the passageway exploded in a series of sharp cracks.

The inner tunnel doors were almost fully open now. Chisnall took a grenade and set the timer to the maximum: sixty seconds. He placed it on the control desk and pulled the pin, then shoved the bay door controls back into the closed position.

He sprinted out into the corridor, only to be greeted by a hail of fire from the entrance. He threw himself back into the control room as chips flew from the stone walls around him, peppering his body armor.

He had two grenades left. One was a flash-bang. He

pulled the pin and watched the safety lever spin away into a corner of the room. He threw it, hard, on an angle against the wall of the corridor so that it bounced off and along toward his attackers. Almost immediately, there was a blast of light and a crack of thunder, and he was moving, diving through the doorway of the control room and rolling across to the corridor opposite. A hard left turn and another short corridor, and the monorail bay was ahead of him. He pulled out his sidearm as he emerged into the bay on the upper observation level. Below him, Monster was climbing over the wreckage toward the closing bay doors. More firing came from behind. He snapped off a couple of quick shots with his pistol, not aiming.

He didn't have enough time. He could see that now. The big metal doors were already half closed and he still had to get down to the platform and past the wreckage. If those doors shut, he would be trapped on the wrong side of them, and the grenade in the control room would make sure that he remained trapped.

Monster was already ducking through the rapidly diminishing gap. Chisnall ran a few meters along the upper level and then hurdled the guardrail. He landed on his back on top of the wreckage and twisted around, sliding down the crumpled top of the car.

At the bottom of the car, a jagged piece of metal snagged his body armor at the elbow, jolting him to a stop. He wrenched it free and hurled himself at the gap in the doors. He managed to get his upper body through the opening and then snatched his legs inside as the gates clanged shut. A clamor of rounds struck the doors with staccato metallic clangs. Then came a dull, distant thump that was almost certainly the frag grenade in the control room.

The Bzadians would have to blow these doors open now.

"What kept you?" Price asked.

"I had to check my e-mail," Chisnall managed, sucking in air. "Status updates, that kind of thing."

Price smiled.

They were inside, Chisnall realized. Inside Uluru. As far as he knew, they were the only humans ever to go there.

A circular tunnel stretched away inside the rock. The tunnel was perfectly round and perfectly straight. Whatever tools the Pukes had used for their tunnel digging, they were very powerful and very accurate. Strip lighting ran the length of the tunnel, fixed to the ceiling at the highest point. It was bright but faded as the tunnel disappeared around a corner. He looked at the walls. Not just perfectly round, but perfectly polished as well. They gleamed like marble.

"It's all gray in here," Wilton said. "Why isn't it red?"

"Uluru is only red on the outside," Chisnall said. "It's rusty."

Wilton clearly didn't believe him, but Chisnall couldn't be bothered explaining.

The monorail line extended out along the floor of the tunnel in front of them. There was no time to wait and admire the view. A banging on the big metal doors sounded behind them.

"Let's go," Chisnall said.

Fleming and Bennett each had one end of the warhead. It was a cylindrical object that, to Chisnall, looked like an oversized waste-disposal unit. Thick black wires emerged from dark gray rectangular boxes on the underside of the device and plugged into the end of it. At the top were two silver tubes, protected by thick metal plates. Metal handles attached to the plates allowed the two of them to share the weight of the warhead, although Bennett was clearly struggling.

"Monster, give them a hand with that," Chisnall said, and Monster took Bennett's side.

"Blow the C4," Wilton said. "Blow it now."

"I can't risk it," Chisnall said. "There's enough explosive up there to bring down the whole tunnel."

Even as he spoke, a series of explosions sounded behind them and a lip of smoke curled through the narrow gap between the doors.

"Sounds like grenades," Price said. "They haven't had time to bring up any demo charges."

"Let's move it," Chisnall said.

The curve in the tunnel was about a hundred meters away. If they could reach that, he would feel safer about blowing the tunnel entrance. They had plenty of time before the aliens could bring up some heavy demo and blow the doors.

He was wrong.

They were barely fifty meters into the tunnel when a booming crash sounded behind them and the big metal doors shuddered.

Chisnall had just enough time to look back in a state of shocked confusion when a second explosion shattered the doors, sending them flying off their hinges into the walls of the tunnel. With the team trapped in the narrow confines of the smooth tunnel walls, the shock wave blasted them off their feet, and Chisnall saw the other Angels go flying, scattered like tenpins.

The rotorcraft. They must have evacuated the area, then used the gunship, hovering outside to blow the outer doors, to fire right through the opening into the bay. There was no need to wait for demo charges when you had a gunship to use instead.

"Blow the entrance!" Price yelled.

Chisnall, in a daze, reached for the detonator at his waist.

It wasn't there.

Shadowy figures were emerging through the smoke and haze behind them, and the air was alive with the crackle of bullets. The walls were exploding in puffs of rock around them.

He saw Bennett go down, hands clutched to his neck, a dark liquid bubbling up between his fingers. He saw Monster start to rise and get hit, flung forward on his face like a rag doll. And then he saw the detonator. It had been knocked from his belt and had fallen into the channel in the middle of the monorail track. Rounds flew around him, punching holes in the dust that filled the air of the tunnel. He tumbled over into the channel, his fingers closing over the detonator. He flicked off the safety.

"Good night," he said, and pressed the trigger.

And then everything was gone.

BOOK 3—ULURU

14. YOZI

[MISSION DAY 5]

[1240 hours]

[Uluru Secure Facility, New Bzadia]

YOZI WAS ON THE FIRST RUNG OF THE LADDER WHEN THE world turned gray.

Zabet was just ahead of him, Alizza right below him.

He and his squad had been detained by Goezlin and his PGZ goons after the prisoner scumbugz had got away, and they had been questioned like criminals—as if they were somehow involved in whatever Chizna was up to.

What *was* Chizna up to? Yozi had no idea. There had been a movement on Bzadia that was opposed to the acquisition of Earth as a new home for the Bzadian race. But they were generally peaceable, nonviolent types who were mainly opposed to the bloodshed inherent in an invasion. It was hard to believe that they had suddenly turned militant and infiltrated the army.

It was also possible that there was some kind of power struggle going on within the army. That had happened before. And possibly Uluru and its powerful secrets could be the cause of the problems. But that didn't quite feel right to him. So the only real possibility that remained was that Chizna and his team were working for the scumbugz. But why?

By the time Goezlin had let them go, they found themselves at the back of a crowd of angry soldiers desperate to get inside the building. The entranceway lay in rubble, blasted by tank shells. The only way in was via two ladders up to the mezzanine floor. That made for slow going.

Yozi had muscled his way to the front of the crowd. Anybody who objected had to argue with Alizza. Nobody did.

He had just put one foot on the ladder when he heard the blast. A second later, the shock wave of broken rock and rubble exploded through the corridor above him. In that second, Alizza saved his life.

Alizza wrenched Yozi off the ladder, throwing him sideways. He dived on top of Yozi as a torrent of dust, rock, and smoke exploded out above them. Chunks of rock crashed down around them. When it finally stopped, Yozi was amazed that he was still alive. He opened his eyes. The first thing he saw across the dust-choked floor was the face of Zabet.

She hadn't been so lucky.

Alizza pushed himself upward, shaking off dust and rock.

Yozi quickly checked Zabet for signs of life, but it was clear there would be none.

He looked at Alizza, then at the pile of rubble in front of them.

They began to climb.

15. DARKNESS AND DUST

[1245 hours]

[Uluru Secure Facility, New Bzadia]

DARKNESS AND DUST. DUST AND DARKNESS.

Chisnall was heaving great clogging balls of dust out of his lungs in gut-wrenching coughs, interspersed with dry heaves. The darkness was absolute. The strip lighting in the tunnel had vanished in the blast. He tried to move his arms. The right one responded, but there was no movement from his left, if it even still existed. He eased his right arm forward and found his combat visor, flipping it up.

He remembered the rag that Monster had given him to hold the hot gun barrel. He found it in a pocket and pulled it out, holding it over his mouth and nose and breathing through it.

For the first time, he got air. Harsh, acrid, smoke-laden

air that smelled of gun oil, but it was air. He hawked and spat, clearing some of the grit from his throat. His water canteen was on his right rear hip. He found it and took a small swig, rinsing it around his mouth and spitting it out before putting the cloth back over his face and drawing another breath.

He was lying mostly on his left side, down in the channel in the monorail track. He rolled onto his stomach, and his left arm suddenly started working again. He must have been lying on it. Pushing himself up onto his elbows and then back onto his knees, he could see absolutely nothing. Nor could he feel anything, but that was a good thing. No pain, at least nothing excruciating, so hopefully no major injuries. Lucky again.

He had a flashlight. He should know which pocket it was in, but his brain felt as thick and heavy as the air in the tunnel. Thoughts and facts tumbled over and swirled around in random patterns. He fumbled until he found the light, and switched it on. Dust particles immediately made a flowing curtain in front of his face. It did not seem as thick now, and somehow he got it into his brain that the dust would be gradually settling. That the higher he got, the less dust there would be.

He stood up, and the air cleared a little more. He stepped up out of the channel onto the monorail track and found that he could breathe without the rag. He shone his flashlight through the swirling dust to the smooth rock walls of the tunnel. There was no sign of his team.

He had been the only one down in the channel, he remembered, and hoped that didn't mean he was the only one who had survived.

Chisnall turned back toward the tunnel entrance, but that was completely gone. All that he could see was a massive pile of rock. The flesh of Uluru.

The smooth walls and ceiling had been replaced by a myriad of cracks and deep fissures. Overhead, a web of fractured rock extended almost to the curve in the tunnel ahead. It looked unstable, an avalanche waiting for a trigger to start its headlong rush down a mountainside.

Still he could see no one.

Had he killed his entire team?

The shock of the explosion was gradually wearing off, and a few connections were starting to flicker together into some sort of reasoning inside his brain.

"Angel Team, response check," he called, fighting off the icy grip of panic that clutched at him.

Silence.

"Angel Team? Angel Team!"

He frantically dived back down into the thick soup of settling dust and scrabbled around with his hands. He could feel only the rubble-coated floor.

"Angel Team!"

He stood and moved forward, sliding his feet across the ground to avoid stepping on anyone.

Still nothing. No one.

Trying not to panic, he took a deep breath, dropped back

to his hands and knees, and felt around through the dust. His hands closed on an ankle.

Chisnall felt his way up the body to the arms and thrust his hands under the shoulders, lifting the person up out of the thick dust. It was Wilton, and he was alive, although breathing shallowly, lips coated with rock dust. Pushing Wilton up against the wall of the tunnel, Chisnall held him there with an arm across his chest. He pulled Wilton's visor back and splashed water over his face. It ran down his chin and neck in gray rivulets. He squeezed Wilton's cheeks together and poured water into his pursed lips. Wilton gagged, choked, and spat, and his eyes opened. He looked weak and groggy.

"Can you stand?" Chisnall asked.

Wilton said nothing, but his eyes turned toward Chisnall.

"Can you stand?"

A weak nod.

"Stay here, stay upright. The dust is thicker down low."

Another weak nod.

Chisnall took another deep breath and plunged back down into the swirling currents of dust. His hand touched body armor, and he hauled Brogan up and repeated the water routine. Once more, and Price was sitting with the others. He heard a cough from behind and found Fleming farther down the tunnel, toward the entrance. He was sitting up, leaning against the tunnel wall.

"Are you okay?" Chisnall asked.

"I'm not sure," Fleming said. "I can't move my legs."

He couldn't move them, Chisnall could see, because a

huge boulder covered them, almost sitting in Fleming's lap. He didn't want to guess what they were going to find underneath that boulder.

The warhead was on the floor, just in front of Fleming. Chisnall checked it quickly. The casing looked intact, so he left it and went back to his search.

Bennett was not far from Fleming, but there was no good news there. He was gone. The dust mixed with a pool of blood around his head to create a red sludge.

The dust was settling more each moment, and although Chisnall was still wading through it, he could see the floor and anyone on it. But there was nobody.

Monster seemed to have completely disappeared.

He felt a hand on his shoulder, and Wilton was there, gray-faced but recovered enough to help. They took opposite sides of the track and trudged forward, feeling with their boots for any obstruction bigger than a loose rock but found nothing.

It wasn't until Chisnall thought of searching the channel that they discovered him, facedown and unmoving in a tumbled pile of rock and a slurry of dust.

"No, not Monster," Wilton breathed from behind Chisnall, echoing his own thoughts.

There was something about Monster that had seemed indestructible, that would just smile in the face of hell and destruction and keep on going. It was shattering to see his cold, still body lying awkwardly in the monorail trench.

"Check his pulse," he said.

Wilton stepped forward but stopped when a dull boom came from behind them, followed by a series of crashes. The pile of rocks at the entrance was shaking.

"They don't waste any time," Wilton said.

The Bzadians were already blasting their way through the rubble.

"We've got to get moving," Chisnall said.

Brogan looked dazed but was standing by herself now, no longer needing the support of the wall.

"Wilton, give me a hand with Fleming," Chisnall said.

They raced back to the SAS man, who was still sandwiched between the rock and the tunnel wall.

"We've got to move that boulder," Chisnall said. He looked around for anything they could use as a lever, but there was nothing but rocks and rubble.

A little reluctantly, he hit the release button for his coilgun and it appeared in his hands. He unhooked it from the holster spring.

Another explosion sounded from the caved-in entrance to the tunnel, and a fractured slab of stone crashed from the ceiling, not far from them. It showered them with more dust and debris.

"You have to leave me here," Fleming said.

"No," Chisnall said.

"You can't jeopardize the mission for one person," Fleming said.

Brogan shook her head, agreeing with Fleming.

"Watch me," was Chisnall's reply.

Wilton helped him move a smaller boulder into place to use as a fulcrum, then used the barrel of the coil-gun as a lever. He leaned on the stock of the gun while Wilton put his shoulder to the rock.

Fleming grunted a little as the weight of the boulder shifted. He must have been in excruciating pain, but the only sound that escaped his lips was that grunt, little more than a whisper of air.

The rock shifted slightly, and the end of the lever slipped a little deeper underneath. Chisnall kicked at the fulcrum stone, shifting it into a better position, then pressed on the lever again. He put the full weight of his body onto it. The coil-gun was tough; it didn't break, although Chisnall doubted that it would ever fire again. Price joined him pushing down on the lever while Wilton braced himself against the tunnel wall. The rock rolled up a bit more, held there for a second by their combined strength, then slowly rolled back to where it had been.

A third explosion came from the tunnel entrance and a low rumble shook the whole tunnel. A large rock, blasted from the pile, hit the ground near them. It tumbled past, so close that Chisnall felt its passage, before it crashed into the channel. A meter to the right and it would have smeared them all down the tunnel wall.

Brogan watched, but made no attempt to help as Chisnall repositioned the rock and the lever and leaned back on the stock of the coil-gun. He looked grimly at Wilton, but Wilton wasn't paying attention; he was looking up the tunnel. Chisnall followed the beam of his flashlight and saw a ghost.

It was a barrel-chested, broad-shouldered, tree-trunk-legged ghost that strode steadily down the tunnel, shedding layers of dust as it came. Monster Panyoczki had somehow taken on Bzadian bullets and the crushing rock of Uluru and won.

"Monster!" It was intended to be a shout, but it came out as a small breath. "Cheese and rice!"

Monster marched up to the boulder without a word, lay down on the floor of the cavern, and put those huge, ham-like legs on the rock. Blood was pouring from a gash in one of his calves, but he didn't seem to notice. He began to push. Chisnall and Wilton leaned back on the lever, and Price positioned herself behind Fleming, ready to slide him out from between the boulder and the wall as soon as the boulder lifted.

The muscles in Monster's legs rippled. The rock moved up the wall, and this time it kept moving. Price pulled Fleming out and was at his legs immediately, probing them with her fingers.

Chisnall examined his weapon. The barrel no longer looked straight, and the shot-counter on the side was cracked. It was now just a dead weight. He tossed it into the dust of the channel, wincing as he did so. If his drill sergeant back at Fort Carson saw how he had treated his weapon, he would have torn strips off him.

"Monster!" Wilton yelled, grabbing one of the handles of the warhead.

Chisnall couldn't resist looking at Monster's back as he lifted one side of the warhead. He had seen him get shot! His body armor showed evidence of three rounds. All of them had hit Monster's coil-gun, which was still holstered across his back. Two of them had ricocheted off into his body armor. It had cracked but held.

Price looked up. "Fleming's going to be okay. His legs were pinned between the rock and the wall, not crushed. I'm no medic, but as far as I can tell, the bones aren't broken."

Chisnall breathed out slowly. He'd had visions of Fleming's legs being flattened like a pancake under the weight of the huge boulder.

"Can you move?"

Fleming nodded.

A series of explosions rumbled from the rockfall behind them as they moved down the tunnel, deeper into Uluru.

16. THE PLATFORM

THEY CAME TO A DOOR THAT WAS DIFFERENT FROM THE others. Different from any door that Chisnall had ever seen. It was perhaps three meters wide, made of six interlocking fingers of steel fitted so snugly together that the join was little more than a hairline.

They stood on the tracks below a monorail platform similar to the one they had found at the entrance to the rock. They had tabbed over half a kilometer along the track to get to this second platform, taking turns carrying the warhead and helping Brogan and Fleming.

The dust storm was gone now. The silence this far inside the rock was absolute, and yet it thundered inside his ears.

To Chisnall, the cold sense of strangeness here was almost overwhelming. The metal fingers of the door seemed to be smiling at him, in an unearthly, lopsided steel grin. Here was danger. Here was evil. For the first time, he wanted to abort the mission. To turn around and escape from this place. Not to have to confront what lay inside.

What kind of abomination had the invaders of his planet hidden under a rock, behind these smirking doors? He thought of the creatures that leered down from the tops of the alien buildings and half wondered if they *were* breeding some giant, mythical chimera monsters to set loose on the human race.

There were monorail cars here. Six of them were parked in a line, just a few meters past the platform. Chisnall glanced back down the tunnel. Part of the roof had collapsed a few moments ago and the aliens had clearly decided to take a more cautious approach to digging through the rubble.

"Looks like you were right," Price said, nodding at the cars.

Chisnall shook off his feeling of terror.

"It made sense," Chisnall said. "There would have to be some way of getting people out quickly in an emergency."

Price looked at the doors. "So all we have to do is stick our head in there and find out what they're up to, then jump on one of those cars and get the hell out of this place."

"Right after we blow them all to hell," Wilton said.

"That's pretty much the plan," Chisnall said. "Now shut it. They'll probably have security cameras and microphones on the platform."

The lights in the tunnel had all gone out when they had blown up the entrance building, but here the platform was brightly lit. For safety, they had left Fleming and Brogan with the warhead, about twenty meters back down the tunnel, well out of sight in the darkness.

A security panel squawked as they approached the doors, and a female voice asked, "What is going on out there?"

Chisnall approached the panel. "I'm Chizna," he said in Bzadian. "I'm with Bomb Disposal. We were attempting to disarm a missile at the entrance to the tunnel when it exploded."

"You're all okay?"

Chisnall couldn't decide whether the voice sounded concerned or suspicious.

"We had enough warning to retreat inside the tunnel," Chisnall said. "But I have two injured soldiers who urgently need medical treatment. And the tunnel is completely blocked. It could be days before they dig it out."

There was a brief silence while the person inside contemplated that.

"My soldiers need urgent medical attention," Chisnall said.

There was a loud hiss and the huge metal fingers of the door slid smoothly apart, sliding back into the rock walls.

No demons appeared. No forces of darkness or dark clouds of evil. In fact, it was quite the opposite. Inside was a plainly decorated entranceway. A bench ran around the walls. It looked like a waiting room in a doctor's office. Perfectly normal. He began to feel a little foolish for his thoughts earlier. But his sense of strangeness did not leave him.

A face peered through the open doorway at the team. It was a woman, smaller than most aliens and possibly the oldest Bzadian Chisnall had ever seen. She wore a guard's uniform that hung loosely over withered shoulders. She smelled old, as if the flesh were already decaying on her not-yet-dead bones.

She looked the team over a couple of times. Chisnall knew how they must appear, bloodied and dusty.

Perhaps she saw something, or perhaps it was just instinct, but something in her eyes showed alarm and she reached back inside. Another hiss and the doors slid smoothly shut, but not before Price hurled herself forward in a single fluid motion, diving and rolling through the closing gap milliseconds before the metal fingers interlocked behind her combat boots.

A second passed, then another, and then the doors slid open again.

Price was standing by the door, her rifle steady in her hands. The woman and another guard, younger and burlier, sat against the wall with their hands clasped on top of their heads.

"What are you doing?" the older guard protested, but Chisnall ignored her and stepped inside. Wilton and Monster followed him.

"Tie them," he ordered, still in Bzadian.

On one side of the doors was a single button. He pressed it and the thick fingers of the door slid smoothly shut. He pressed it again, and they opened just as smoothly.

Oval-shaped passageways led off the curved walls of the room in three directions. One to the left, one to the right, and one straight ahead. Doors were also to their left and right. The one to the left was open.

While Price and Wilton secured the two guards, Chisnall glanced through the open doorway. In a small room, little more than a cupboard, two chairs faced a bank of security screens. A tall tube of a steaming liquid sat on a table, next to a half-eaten food roll. It was clearly the guards' station.

There were four screens altogether. Two showed views of the platform outside the door, from different angles. The others were blank. Chisnall guessed they had previously shown views of the main entrance building, but the cameras had been destroyed in the blast.

Monster opened a door on the right of the atrium. Chisnall walked over to investigate. It was dark inside, but Monster found a switch and the room flooded with light, revealing a storeroom.

"Put the guards in here," Chisnall said. "Then watch the entrances while we get Brogan and Fleming."

He turned back to the doors and to his surprise found the warhead sitting on the platform and Brogan helping Fleming to climb up. The spark in her eyes was back.

"Holly!" He tried to keep the relief in his voice from being too obvious. "How are you feeling? You're okay?"

"Got one helluva headache," she said, "but everything seems to be functioning."

"Great," Chisnall said. He extended a hand to Fleming to help him up. "How's the leg?"

"Like a rabid dog is chewing on the bone," Fleming said, "but it's good to have some feeling back in it. I can walk."

"We were just coming back for you," Chisnall said. "How long will it take you to arm this thing?"

He took one side of the warhead, Fleming took the other, and they moved it off the platform into the entranceway.

"No time at all," Fleming said. "Just punch in a time and hit the button."

"Okay. Let's recon this place. See if we can find an answer for HQ about what's going on in here. Then we press the big bang button and get clear."

"I don't think so."

It was Brogan who had spoken, behind him on the platform. Chisnall turned. She looked focused, determined.

So did the sidearm that she pointed directly at Chisnall's face.

"What the hell, Brogan?" Wilton asked, his coil-gun leaping over his shoulder into his hands.

"Put it away," Brogan said. "Unless you want to see what the skipper's brains look like."

"Put the gun away, Wilton," Chisnall said. "There's no need."

"What are you doing?" Price asked.

"Her job," Chisnall said. "She's been working for the Bzadians all along. She sabotaged my half-pipe and the laser comm unit. And she killed Hunter."

Wilton swore at her. Brogan's pistol didn't waver. Her face was expressionless.

"You knew?" she asked.

"Of course," Chisnall said.

"And you did nothing?"

"That's not entirely true," Chisnall said. "I did take out your sidearm's battery and replace it with a dead one."

Brogan instinctively turned the gun sideways to check the battery meter. It only took a second, but it was long enough. Chisnall punched her hand sideways and dived forward, knocking her backward and down. She tried to bring the gun back to bear, but he had his full weight on top of her. Then a sharp boot from Price kicked the gun out of her hands.

Both Price and Wilton had their coil-guns aimed at her head now.

Chisnall twisted her onto her stomach. He found a cord in a utility pocket and bound her hands securely, then let her sit back up.

"How did you know it was me?" she asked, breathing heavily.

"I didn't, until just now," he said. "In fact, I thought it was probably Price."

"Bite me," Price said.

Chisnall sat back on his haunches and looked at her. "Why, Holly?" he asked.

"I don't have to say anything," she said.

"Why would a human help aliens?"

"For reasons you'll never understand," she spat.

"This is our planet. You're siding with the enemy."

"*You* are the enemy," she said.

"Chisnall, we need to get moving," Fleming said.

Chisnall looked at her for a moment longer, then shook his head.

"Bring her," he said. "Price, you're in charge of her. Watch her carefully."

He unclipped Brogan's coil-gun from her back holster and handed it to Fleming.

Chisnall and Monster retrieved the warhead from the platform; then Chisnall shut the doors again. Sealing them in and the enemy out.

"Which way?" Wilton asked.

"No idea. You pick."

Wilton picked the first passageway to the right. It led to a heavy metal door. Chisnall nodded at him to try the handle. It wasn't locked.

Guns at the ready, they pushed open the door and eased their way into the room. Large generators hummed and the walls were lined with fuel cells. That explained the bright lights in the facility, while the rest of the tunnel was blacked out.

"Good place for a warhead," Monster said.

"Agreed," Chisnall said. "Those fuel cells will go up like the Fourth of July."

Monster and Wilton each took one side of the warhead, moving it into the generator room. After a little looking around, they hid it in a gap between one of the generators and a wall, moving an empty fuel cell in front of it for further concealment.

They moved back to the entrance.

Chisnall found a square of card and began to sketch a quick map of the complex.

"Your turn to pick," Wilton said, looking at the remaining passageways.

Chisnall was about to choose the passageway to the left, at random, when the decision was made for them. A Bzadian walked out of the front passageway. He was holding a steaming drink tube.

He took in the scene—the human and the coil-gun in Price's hands that was rising up toward him—and reacted instantly, flinging the drink tube at Price's face. He spun on his heels as she twisted away from the burning liquid. The Bzadian raced back down the short passageway and out of sight. A moment later, an alarm started blaring and a red light in the ceiling started flashing.

"Damn," Price said.

"Doesn't change a thing," Chisnall said. "Let's get on with what we came here to do."

He took a breath and then turned to Fleming. "Get yourself into that security office and keep an eye on the monitors. If the Pukes manage to dig through that rubble, I want to know about it."

Fleming nodded and limped off to the left.

"Okay, we're Oscar Mike," Chisnall said. "Stay frosty. Let's recon this place as quickly as we can, set the timer on the warhead, then make like a bunch of birds."

"And flock off," Wilton finished the old joke.

Chisnall took his sidearm in a two-handed police-style

grip. He scanned the middle passageway before crouching and stepping into it.

It was no more than six meters long, if that. At the end, it turned sharply right and led into a long room.

"Check your corners," Chisnall said, although it seemed an odd thing to say in a room where there were no corners. The aliens' fondness for rounded architecture extended underground, and the room they were in had only sweeping curves.

The room was actually more of a long hall. They could see the end, but it seemed far away in the distance. It was dimly lit, with globes in groupings of three on the ceiling. About halfway down, a red alarm light was flashing—it washed the room intermittently with a bloodlike glow. On the left side were doorways, one after another, evenly spaced. Small shrubs in circular tubs added a little green to this stark dungeon.

Every shrub was a hiding place. Every doorway down the long hall was a potential sniper's nest.

"What the hell is this place?" Wilton asked.

Nobody else spoke.

The alarm siren echoed off the long walls, bouncing back to them in a solid wall of sound.

"Where are all the Pukes?" Price asked.

"Wilton, Monster." Chisnall nodded at the first door.

Price pressed Brogan against a wall, her gun at the back of her neck.

"If I even think you're going to call out, I'll make sure you can't. Permanently," Price said.

Chisnall crouched down, weapons aimed forward down the long hall. Wilton and Monster took the doorway assault-style. They flattened themselves against each side of the door before smashing it open with a boot heel and diving inside—one left, one right, one high, one low—guns ready.

"Clear," Wilton said, and Monster echoed the word. The room was empty.

They disappeared inside for a moment, then reappeared.

"It's a dorm," Wilton said. "Bzadian style. Eight sleeping tablets. Empty."

"Lived in?" Chisnall asked.

Wilton nodded. "Clothes, personal effects. Lights are on but nobody's home."

The next doorway was the same, and the next. Wherever the inhabitants of this place were, it was not in their living quarters.

Halfway along the hall, light from a side passage fell in a pool on the floor. After a quick sweep of the remaining dormitories, they made their way back to the lighted passage.

As they neared it, the red flash and strident siren stopped abruptly.

"It was giving me a headache," Fleming's voice said on the comm.

"Good effort," Chisnall said.

The passage was ten meters long with a door at the end. Closed, but there was no lock.

Chisnall pulled down on the handle as quietly as he could and used the snout of his sidearm to push the door open.

Silence. No shots. No shouting.

He eased it open a fraction more, then looked back at his team. "Okay. Who wants to be a hero?" he asked.

Nobody answered.

"It's you," Chisnall said, looking at Wilton.

Wilton grinned and took a step backward. The others cleared a path. He broke into a run, and just as he reached the door, Chisnall flicked it open. Wilton rolled through the doorway in a crouch—the smallest possible target. He scanned the room while the others leaned out from the doorway to offer fire support.

Two large machines took most of the space. From one came the sound of rushing water and from the other the sound of flowing air. This would be the plant room that kept air and water circulating throughout the underground installation.

Still no contact with the enemy.

Chisnall examined his rough map of the underground complex. "Let's start again from the beginning," he said.

They returned to the passageway and walked through the accommodation block back to the entrance.

"Anything on the monitors?" Chisnall asked.

"All clear," Fleming said.

Chisnall checked his map, marking in the doors and passageways that led out from the atrium.

First door on the left, the security office.

First door on the right, the storeroom.

First passageway on the right led to the generator room where they had hidden the warhead.

The middle door was the passage to the dormitories.

That left the second passage on the left.

"On me," he said, and led the way into it. Price came last, pushing Brogan along in front of her.

It opened into an office area. A circular room. The desks were workstations, four chairs at each, with a low partition allowing the users some privacy while they worked. Admin staff, Chisnall guessed. The desks were made of a light, aluminum-like metal that the Bzadians used extensively.

The computers and filing cabinets might yield interesting data, he thought, but there was little time to stop and investigate. Several of the desks were covered with pieces of paper. Tables of numbers and charts.

"Still warm," Price said. Chisnall looked over to see her pressing the back of her hand to a drinking tube on one of the desks.

The aliens had cleared out in a hurry.

"We'll come back here after the preliminary recon," he said. "See what we can get out of those computers."

So far they had found little of interest. Yet the aliens had gone to a lot of trouble to hide this place away from satellite eyes, deep inside Uluru. They had done that for a reason.

They passed through the administration offices, weapons ready. The Pukes had to be somewhere. But where?

They took the passageway directly in front of them, emerging into a mess hall. Some of the tables still had food and drinking tubes on them. A music keyboard was near one wall, a Bzadian-style electronic piano with a circle of wedge-shaped buttons emanating from a central hub. Some wilted decorations were stuck to the walls around it. There had been a celebration of some kind in here, but now it was deserted.

"Where the hell is everybody?" Wilton asked.

"Maybe they've got a panic room," Price said.

That would make sense, Chisnall thought. A safe room where the Pukes would have headed as soon as they heard the alarm. That would explain why every room they found was deserted.

They passed a kitchen, also deserted, although some large pots still steamed. A passageway at the end of the hall took them to restrooms with circular Bzadian-style toilets and wash cubicles. That was a dead end, except for a short passage back to the dormitories, so they backtracked to the administration center.

They had finally come to the last door. Every other room and passageway had been searched. Whatever secret Uluru had to reveal, it was behind this door.

Would it be worth it? Chisnall wondered. All the danger. All the risk.

Would it be worth Hunter?

He looked at his team. They were poised and ready.

He looked at Brogan.

He took a deep breath and pushed open the door.

It led to a large room with benches running around the outside walls and computer workstations in the center. A closed door blocked the way forward.

The strangeness was upon him once again.

"Stay frosty," he murmured.

The team took up assault positions around the door.

The door opened inward, so Chisnall eased it open while the others trained their weapons on the gap.

They were greeted by silence and darkness.

From the air in the room, Chisnall felt it was large, but he could not see the end, nor the ceiling, not even the sides—except where a small beam of light from the open doorway illuminated the walls.

"Get out of the doorway," he said. Silhouetted by the light from the lab, his team would make perfect targets for anyone inside.

The Angels split to either side, out of the firing line.

"Wilton, on me," Chisnall said. "Everyone else, hang back, give us cover."

He moved forward and shone his flashlight around the walls. It reflected back at him off glass surfaces, making it impossible to see what lay on the other side.

Wilton moved behind him, searching the darkness.

There was no light switch that he could see.

"See if the lights are controlled from the lab," he called back through the doorway.

A moment later Monster said, "Got it."

There was a click and a series of fluorescent lights flickered above them, creating a harsh strobelike effect for a moment. Then the lights came on fully, bursting into brilliant incandescent life. They revealed another long chamber with rounded corners, narrower than some of the other rooms, little more than a wide passageway. On either side, glass walls covered a series of cubicles that ran the length of the wall.

And in those cubicles was the truth about Uluru.

"Holy shit," Chisnall said. His voice sounded far-off and distant.

Wilton said nothing as Chisnall lowered his weapon.

"You'd better get in here, guys," he said.

He walked to the nearest cubicle and put his hand on the glass wall. It was actually a door, he realized, rubberized around the edges, with a long metal strip hinge that ran from top to bottom on the right-hand side. Gleaming white walls and harsh lighting gave the cubicle the appearance of a hospital room or a morgue. Inside the cubicle was a bed: a hard, narrow, rubberized mattress on a dull metal frame.

On the bed was a human.

A woman.

Naked.

With tubes running in and out of her body.

The woman appeared to be conscious but didn't look at Chisnall as he approached the glass. Her eyes were unfocused, dull. The world outside the cubicle did not seem to exist for her.

Her hair was cropped so short that it might as well have been shaved.

And she was pregnant.

17. CELLS

CHISNALL FLIPPED UP HIS COMBAT VISOR, SUDDENLY needing air.

Thoughts of an ambush were gone for the moment. Thoughts of the outside world vanished. There was only Uluru. This cavern. The glass-fronted cubicles. It was as if his entire world had been reduced to a small bubble.

Each cubicle was the same. A glass-fronted prison cell. In each, a woman: vacant, staring, impaled by the cold plastic of the tubes worming into her naked body. The women all appeared to be in their twenties. Their skin was pale, unpigmented and unblemished by the sun of the outside world.

One moved as he passed her cell, and he pressed himself to the glass, convinced that she had just made an effort to look at him. But her eyes were unseeing, and she didn't react when he tapped on the glass. A bubble of saliva drooled out of her mouth. It hung from the edge of her lip for a moment before stretching into a long string and collecting in a small pool on the gray rubber of the mattress.

"What the hell is this?" Wilton asked, right behind him, making him jump.

"Is like a farm," Monster said.

Monster was right, Chisnall thought. It did look like a farm, like battery hens. But it wasn't eggs they were laying. It was babies. This was the dirty secret of Uluru.

He looked at Brogan. She looked shocked, and he didn't think she was faking it. She hadn't known about this room.

He eased himself back from the cell and looked toward the end of the cavern. He forced himself to focus. They were on a mission. He was the leader. He had to command. But all he could see was this horror. This inhumanity. Human beings reduced to breeding animals. And why? What reason could the aliens have for doing this?

The women were in various stages of pregnancy, but there seemed to be some kind of order to it. The most pregnant women were closest to the lab. As he walked away from the lab, the size of the swelling in the women's stomachs reduced.

"This isn't right," Wilton said. "Where did they get the women from?"

"In a war, people disappear every day," Chisnall said.

"And who got them pregnant?" Wilton asked.

"Who knows," Chisnall said. "Artificially inseminated, probably."

"By humans?" Wilton asked, and a dreadful silence fell over the room.

"Cross-breeds," Price murmured. "Chimeras."

"We don't know that," Chisnall said.

He walked to the back of the group and grabbed Brogan by the back of the neck, pushing her face into the glass of the nearest cell.

"What's going on in here?" he asked, trying and failing to restrain the fury that exploded from somewhere deep within his brain.

Her nose began to bleed. The blood ran down the front of the glass.

"Are you cross-breeding humans and Bzadians?" he asked.

"No," she gasped, spitting out blood. "No, not that."

"Then what?"

She was silent.

"Maybe they're studying the human development cycle," Price said. "Trying to develop a weapon that will stop humans from reproducing."

"Then we all die out and the planet is theirs," Monster said.

Chisnall looked around at them, his gaze finally coming to rest on Brogan, blood covering her lips and chin. He was losing it, he knew, and he shut his eyes briefly, trying to get on top of his emotions. Was it the horror of what they had just found or the feeling of betrayal? Either way he had to act professionally.

He let go of Brogan, who slumped to the floor.

"Maybe you're right," he said to Price and Monster, without clarifying who he thought was right. Did it really matter?

"What's that noise?" Wilton asked.

Chisnall heard it too. A sluicing sound, like water through pipes. Tiny nozzles in the ceiling of the cells burst into life, dispensing a soapy solution. The women below automatically shut their eyes and mouths as the spray soaked them. Another spray rinsed the soap from their bodies.

"Like a car wash," Monster said, which was exactly what Chisnall had been thinking.

"This place gives me the creeps," Wilton said.

"Everybody focus," Chisnall said. "The Pukes are still around somewhere. Let's finish this recon and get the heck out of here."

"What about the warhead, Lieutenant?" Price asked.

He looked at the woman in the cubicle nearest him. The wide, staring eyes, the drooling mouth. What had they done to her? They had turned her into little more than a test tube.

But she was still human.

He keyed his comm switch. "Fleming, what's the status on the warhead?"

"Just let me know when you want the big bang, and I'll set the timer," Fleming said.

"We can't do that now."

"Can't do what now?"

"Detonate the warhead."

"Why is that, Lieutenant?"

"There are human beings in here," Chisnall said. He described the scene to Fleming.

"Copy that," Fleming said. "In that case, finish your recon, and let's bug out of here before the Pukes break through that rock pile."

He had answered a little too quickly, Chisnall thought. But there was no time to dwell on what that might mean.

"Okay, we are Oscar Mike," he said.

The passageway at the end of the room took them to a nursery where long rows of plastic boxes—incubators—sat on frames under soft lights. Above each incubator, a cantilevered arm held a lamp.

Chisnall eyed one curiously.

"Ultraviolet lights," Price said.

The incubators were empty.

They did not delay in the nursery. A passageway at the end took them back into the dormitories.

"Back to the entrance," Chisnall said. "Fleming's right. It's time we got out of here."

But he stopped after a few meters. A side passage appeared in the wall to the left, and through it he could see rows of chairs and tables.

"Hold up," he said. "A quick look in here first."

It was a classroom. It was set up with SMART boards, desks, chairs, and a globe of the world in a corner. It looked just like any classroom in any school in the world. Any *human* school.

"Just like immersion camp," Monster said.

Chisnall gaped at him.

The last year of their training at Fort Carson, they had been in immersion camp. They lived in a Bzadian-style dormitory. They spoke only Bzadian and ate Bzadian food. They lived, breathed, and even dreamed Bzadian. It was all designed to prepare them for infiltrating Bzadian society.

"No, not just like. It *is* an immersion camp," Chisnall said. He looked back at Brogan. She glared at him.

"What are you saying, LT?" Wilton asked.

"Maybe that's what this is all about," Chisnall said. "Maybe they're not cross-breeding species or designing some supervirus to wipe us all out. Maybe they're growing spies."

"What?" Wilton said.

"It makes sense," Chisnall said. "They breed human children, train them to infiltrate human society. They're preparing them for the human world the same way we were prepared for the Bzadian world. That explains the baby factory back there. It explains the school. It explains . . ." His voice trailed off.

"Explains what?" Price asked.

"Brogan."

They all turned to stare at her.

"Brogan's sixteen," Wilton said. "This hasn't been built that long."

"Maybe she's from an earlier batch," Chisnall said.

He looked around at the faces of his team. They had all flipped up their visors and the sharp light of the overhead fluorescents shone through the glass of the visors and made patterns on their faces. Price's lip was curling up in disgust. Wilton looked sad. Monster's face, as usual, showed no emotion.

"The Pukes' greatest weakness in this war is their lack of intel," Chisnall said. "They don't have satellites and they don't have spies in the Free Territories. If I'm right, this project could change all that."

He turned to Brogan. "How many of you are there?" he asked. "How many have already infiltrated the Free Territories?"

She stared at him without expression and said nothing.

"LT," Monster said, looking at the back of the classroom.

Chisnall followed his gaze to another door. He tried the handle—locked.

What more secrets did this rock have to reveal?

"Blow the lock," he said.

Wilton was already pulling a length of det cord out of his backpack.

Chisnall walked around the schoolroom while he waited for Wilton to set the charge. The desks were plastic, as his had been at school. This was clearly designed to mimic as closely as possible the real-world environment that these kids would find themselves in, even down to graffiti on the desks. Scrawled names and pictures of animals and airplanes.

But where were all the kids?

"Fire in the hole," Wilton said.

A flash and a bang and the door sprang open, smashing back into the wall behind.

"Cheese and rice," Monster said.

This was the playground to go with the school. What looked remarkably like blue sky shone overhead, and underfoot was a thick mat of grass. It was set up as a baseball diamond, although a set of moveable soccer goals at each end made it a multipurpose field. To the right was a tennis court and to the left a roped-off area full of gym equipment.

And crowded against the back wall, behind the soccer goal, were children.

Their ages ranged from about five up to perhaps twelve or thirteen. There were boys and girls, all of varying heights and hair colors. They looked just like the kids you would see on any street of any country in the world, playing in front yards, kicking balls across the road.

Chisnall took in the wide, staring eyes of the innocent-looking faces.

These kids could walk through Times Square and no one would give them a second glance.

Human children, raised by Bzadians to betray their own species.

Around the edges of the large, oval room were a bunch of Bzadians in a variety of uniforms and clothing that meant nothing to Chisnall. There must have been at least fifty of them. Probably the scientists and administrators who ran the facility.

"Lieutenant." Fleming's voice broke into his thoughts. "Movement in the monorail tunnel. Pukes, and lots of them."

18. CHINA LAKE

CHISNALL FELT A RISING PANIC. HE FORCED IN A DEEP breath and let it out slowly, humming quietly. He shut his eyes for a moment and banished the fear to the recesses of his mind.

If ever there was a time for clear thinking, this was it.

The Bzadians had found their way into the monorail tunnel much faster than he could have anticipated, and that meant their escape route was gone. The platform and entrance were blocked. There was no other way out of the rock. They were trapped.

"Don't let them in," he said. "This party is invitation only."

"Chisnall." It was Fleming's voice again.

"Yes?"

"I thought you should know. I've armed the warhead."

"Please confirm your last," Chisnall said.

"I have armed the warhead."

"Fleming, disarm it, immediately," Chisnall said.

There was a pause.

"I'm afraid I can't do that, Lieutenant," Fleming said.

"I am ordering you to disarm it," Chisnall said.

He watched Brogan's face as he said it, and her look of horror was unmistakable.

"Lieutenant, your mission was to find out what was inside Uluru. My mission was to destroy it, if I thought it necessary. I think it's necessary. Your mission authority ran out the moment we got inside this rock."

Chisnall found his eyes drawn to the faces of the young children in front of him.

"Fleming, this facility is full of humans. Adults and children. If that warhead explodes, they will all be killed." He added as an afterthought, "And so will we."

"I know," Fleming said.

"Then what the heck do you think you're doing?"

"Millions more people will be killed if the Pukes win this war. Maybe the entire human race, for all we know. If the Pukes manage to infiltrate our society, our military, we won't stand a chance."

"Fleming . . . ," Chisnall began, trying to muster an argument. The problem was, Fleming was right.

"As for you and me," Fleming said, "we were always expendable."

"Nothing ever changes," Price muttered.

"Anyway," Fleming said, "with half the Bzadian Army just about to batter down the doors, we're not going to live through this anyway. If I've gotta go, I'm taking this place with me."

"Fleming . . ." Chisnall hesitated again. "I repeat, there are women and children in here. Human women and children."

"Collateral damage," Fleming said.

"Do you have any humanity?" Chisnall seethed.

"Do you have what it takes to be a soldier?" was Fleming's response.

Chisnall looked around the team. Monster's face was calm, impassive. Wilton's face was a tightly controlled mask. Only Price seemed affected, looking around at the faces of the children with horror in her eyes, although she said nothing.

Chisnall flipped his comm off. "I'm going to talk to him. See if I can change his mind."

"Where's Brogan?" Wilton asked.

There was only one place Brogan would go. Massed in the tunnel were hordes of Bzadian soldiers. If she let them in, it was all over.

Chisnall ran. Monster ran alongside him.

"Fleming!" Chisnall yelled, but there was no answer. "Fleming, Brogan's loose. She's probably heading toward the entrance. Don't let her get near that door!"

There was no answer.

[1440 hours]
[Uluru Secure Facility, New Bzadia]

Yozi fumed, staring down the tunnel, as if by doing so he could hurry things up.

"What's keeping them?" Alizza asked. He took off his helmet and felt the bandage that covered his forehead. It was already sodden with blood from his head wound, but he didn't seem to care as long as it didn't get into his eyes.

Yozi looked at his big friend and clicked his teeth in frustration. Around them, the heavily armed soldiers of the 2nd Assault Battalion shuffled their feet or checked their weapons. They looked angry.

Movement at last. Light at the far end of the tunnel quickly grew into three PGZ goons carrying flashlights and surrounding a small, frightened-looking technician.

The technician was carrying a black metal briefcase, clutching it in front of him as if his life depended on it. It probably did, Yozi thought. He extended a hand and helped the tech up onto the platform but did not offer the same courtesy to the PGZ.

"How long will it take?" Yozi asked.

"J-just a few minutes," the technician stammered. "I need to override the locking codes."

"Then get on with it."

The technician opened the briefcase to reveal a keyboard and screen. He pulled out a cable that had been coiled on top of the keyboard, then handed the briefcase to Yozi to hold while he flipped up the cover on a computer port in the doors and plugged the cable in.

He pressed a key on the keyboard, and the screen came to life.

[1445 hours]
[Uluru Secure Facility, New Bzadia]

Monster kicked open a door and they bounced and skidded their way through a short tunnel to the atrium.

"How do I disarm it?" they heard Brogan shout.

Somehow she had removed her restraints. Brogan had Fleming on the floor, her knee on his back. She had taken her coil-gun back from him, and it was now firmly planted in his ear.

When she noticed Monster and Chisnall racing for her, she sprang off Fleming and leaped toward the control panel, her hand outstretched to hit the button that would open the doors and release the waiting hordes of Bzadians.

Chisnall hurled himself forward, but there was no way he was ever going to make it in time.

Her index finger was just about to connect with the button when the panel exploded into shards of metal and plastic.

Brogan grunted in pain and snatched her hand back, droplets of blood spraying from her fingers.

Her other hand, the one holding her gun, began to rise

toward Chisnall. But he got there first, brushing her arm aside as his body slammed into hers, flattening her up against the wall.

She managed to hang on to her gun and tried again to angle it toward him. He grasped her wrist and smashed it into the wall once, twice, until the gun came loose. She struggled, clawing at him, trying to twist away. Then Monster and Fleming were there. They grabbed her arms and pinned her to the floor.

"Great shot," Fleming said, looking at the shattered control panel.

"Not so much," Monster said. "I was aiming at Brogan."

She gave him an evil look. Chisnall helped hold her while Monster secured her arms behind her back with a metal tie. She wouldn't wriggle out of that.

"What's happening outside?" Chisnall asked.

Fleming rolled away from them and stuck his head into the security office.

"They're still trying to get the door open, as far as I can tell."

"Okay. Fleming, you have to disarm the warhead."

"I'm not going to," Fleming said. "You're trying to save a few lives. I'm trying to save the human race."

There was a silence. Chisnall stared at the floor for a moment, then looked up.

"How long till it explodes?"

"I set it for an hour," Fleming said. He checked his watch. "We have fifty-three mikes left."

Monster had taken a couple of grenades off his belt. He secured them to the door, linking the safety pins together so that when the doors slid open, it would pull the pins out of the grenades.

"Welcome to Uluru," he said.

"What are you going to do, Lieutenant?" Fleming asked.

"I don't know. But for a start, let's get out of here," Chisnall said.

He grabbed Brogan by the arm, wrenching her to her feet. She tried to shake him off, but Monster took her other arm and forced her along with them.

Fleming picked up her coil-gun and followed.

"This way." Chisnall led them into the administration area.

He let go of Brogan's arm and faced her, staring into her eyes until she dropped her gaze.

"Let her go," he said.

Monster did and stepped back a pace. Brogan glowered at Chisnall but said nothing.

"Untie her," Chisnall said.

Monster looked at him carefully. Fleming asked, "Are you sure?"

Chisnall nodded.

Monster reached behind her and cut the metal tie with his knife. She rubbed her wrists where the metal had cut into them.

"Sit down," Chisnall said.

She sat.

He pulled up a chair and sat opposite her, then pulled out

a gauze pad from his medipack and reached for her hand, which was still dripping blood.

"Do we have time for this?" she asked.

"We have all the time in the world," Chisnall said. "In less than an hour, that warhead is going to turn this place into dust. But we won't care, because the Pukes will be through that door in a minute, and we won't survive that. So we may as well just sit here and wait to die."

"If in a few minutes I'm going to be smeared all over that wall, why bother with my hand?"

"I guess it passes the time," he said.

She let him clean and bandage her fingers without further resistance and checked his work with a trained medic's eye when he had finished.

"I'm right, aren't I?" he said. "About this place. The Pukes are growing their own little humans to infiltrate human society."

She said nothing.

"We're about to die," he said. "You might as well tell me the truth. I get it about Uluru, but I don't understand *you*. This facility is, what, maybe ten years old? You're sixteen. How does that work?"

She shrugged. "I was one of the first. From the original experiments. I was brought here when I was five. I can't remember anything before that."

Chisnall thought about that for a moment. "We didn't see any kids younger than about five," he said.

"No. Newborn babies are taken out into the community to live with Bzadian families. We all grow up thinking we're Bzadian. Some don't even realize they look different. When we turn five, we're brought back to Uluru for training."

"Brogan." Chisnall stopped, unsure how to continue. "You were raised by Pukes, but you're not a Puke. Does that not register with you at all?"

"We are going to save the planet," Brogan said. "You humans have been destroying it for centuries. When you're gone, it will be a cleaner, better place."

"That's propaganda your masters have fed you to justify the invasion. The truth is, the Pukes just want the planet for themselves."

Brogan shook her head.

"You're a human being," Chisnall said. "You've lived among us. You know we're not perfect, but are we all that bad? They've brainwashed you since the time you were born to think like them. To go against your own species. But now is the time to wake up. Look around you. You've seen the baby factory."

That got a reaction. She stiffened slightly and shut her eyes.

"You grew up here. You must have known what they were doing to those women," he pressed.

"I didn't know," she said. "We were never allowed in that room. Those women are . . ." Her voice trailed off.

"One of them, or one like them, is your mother," Chisnall said.

Brogan's jaw tightened but her eyes opened slowly, awash with unshed tears.

"Holly, I don't know what they told you about humans, but you know the truth. You know us." Chisnall paused. "You know me."

Now the tears fell.

"What's happening, guys?" It was Wilton's voice on the comm.

"Hold fast," Chisnall said. "We're about to get company."

"Brogan." He reached out and took her hand. She resisted at first, but then let him hold it.

"I'm not your friend, Ryan. I'm your enemy," she said.

"So it was all part of a plan?" he asked. "Get close to the team leader so you could dig up more information?"

"No," she said, and her face hardened as if she was trying to hold back some strong emotion. "They wouldn't have allowed that. In case it made it difficult for me to do what I had to do. And it did."

Chisnall nodded. "You and I are on opposite sides. If I could change your mind, I would. But there's one thing we agree on: we don't want to see all those women and children killed when the warhead goes off."

"They're innocent. That would be murder," Brogan whispered.

"I'm not arguing," Chisnall said. "But I don't think you're going to convince Fleming. You grew up in this place. Is there any other way out? Any emergency exits? Anything like that?"

"Promise you'll take the kids."

"So there *is* a way out?"

"All of them, Ryan."

Fast tears began rolling down her cheeks.

"I promise we'll try." Chisnall sat back in the chair and said nothing more. He let go of her hand and let her sit there, alone, suddenly small and vulnerable.

"There's an air shaft," she said at last.

"Where?"

"From the plant room. It runs up to the surface. It comes out in the cleft."

Chisnall tried to visualize that. On top of Uluru was a huge cleft, almost a valley, that ran down to join one of the gaps between the "toes" of the giant foot.

"Is it big enough to get through?"

She nodded. "You can crawl through it." She stopped and looked at Fleming. "*We* could crawl through it. A human adult probably not."

Fleming's expression did not change.

"There are grilles, air filters, but they can be opened, if you know how," Brogan said. "I've been through it. Me and some of the others. We wanted to see the outside world."

"Does it run straight up?" Fleming asked. "That would be a hell of a climb."

"Only part of it," Brogan said. "And there are rungs. They need to clean the air filters occasionally. Most of it is on a steep angle, but you can crawl it."

"Will you show us?" Chisnall asked.

She looked at the ground for a moment, then nodded. "You've promised you will save those kids, Ryan."

"I won't go back on my word," Chisnall said. "I want to save them as much as you do."

There was a shout from the entrance and the sound of running boots, followed almost immediately by the twin cracks of Monster's grenade booby trap.

19. THE SHAFT

"GO!" CHISNALL YELLED, PUSHING BROGAN UP OUT of her chair. Monster grabbed her arm and pulled her with him.

Fleming didn't move.

Chisnall stopped at the doorway that led to the science labs and looked back.

"I won't fit—you heard that," Fleming said.

"But—"

"Get out of here," Fleming said. "I'll do what I can to give you more time. Here, you're going to need this." He handed Brogan's coil-gun to Chisnall, then moved behind a desk and aimed his own weapon at the doorway. "See you in another life."

Chisnall didn't stop to argue any further.

"Wilton," Chisnall yelled on the comm as they ran through the lab. "Get the Pukes to lie down on the floor with their hands on their heads. Get the kids in a group. We're heading in your direction."

Behind he heard the sound of firing—Fleming engaging the enemy. Pinning them down in the entranceway.

"What's going on?" Wilton asked.

"There's an exit in the plant room, an air shaft," Chisnall yelled. "We're going to try and get the women and kids out of here before the warhead goes off."

"How long have we got?"

"Maybe forty mikes," Chisnall said. He heard a muffled curse on the other end of the comm.

They reached the maternity ward, and he raced to the first cell, examining the glass door. It was locked, but he hammered on the glass with the butt of his sidearm until it shattered. He knocked out the jagged pieces of broken glass and climbed through into the chamber.

"Ma'am, we'd like to take you home," he said.

The staring eyes didn't even turn to look at him.

He touched her face, and she responded to the touch, turning as if to look at him, but her eyes remained unfocused.

"Ryan, they've done"—Brogan stopped and dropped her eyes—"*we've* done something to these women's brains. They're not much more than vegetables. They can't walk and they sure as hell can't climb a ventilation shaft."

"They're humans too," Chisnall said.

"Leave them, Ryan. Help me save the kids," she said.

She was right. He knew she was right. But that didn't make it *right*.

With a last look backward, he climbed out of the cell and ran with the others. As they ran through the empty nursery, he hit the release on his coil-gun and it sprang into his arms. Ahead of him, Monster had done the same.

The sound of Fleming's gunfire came from the hallway behind them as they burst into the schoolroom. Then there was an explosion, and the gunfire was silenced. Fleming had done what he could. But now there was nothing to hold back the angry Puke army.

"Monster, get back to the first dorm," Chisnall said. "It's the only way in. Anything comes that way, shoot it."

He ran into the recreation room. The adult Bzadians were nowhere to be seen, but terrified children huddled by the doorway.

"Where are the others?" Chisnall asked.

"Found a storeroom for gym equipment at the back." Wilton grinned. "Stuck 'em all in there and told them there was a grenade attached to the outside door handle."

"Is there?"

"Nope. Didn't want to waste a grenade."

"Okay, go help Monster." Chisnall turned to Brogan. "Get the kids out of here. We'll try and hold the Pukes off as long as we can. Price, go with them. Watch her. If you think she's trying anything, shoot her."

"Gladly," Price said.

Chisnall reached up to his left shoulder and unclipped the ID tube. He handed it to Price. "This is my data recorder. It's recorded everything we've done or said over the last few days. It has a built-in transmitter. As soon as you're out, press here to trigger it. We have to get this information back to base. And it's our ride home. They'll use the transmitter to find us."

She tucked it into a pocket and turned to the kids.

"Price," Chisnall said.

She glanced back.

"I'm sorry that I thought it was you. That I didn't trust you. It was just . . ."

She shook her head. "Get us out of here alive and all is forgiven."

Chisnall nodded, then ran back to the long dormitory.

Monster and Wilton had taken up defensive positions. Monster was in one of the doorways; Wilton was crouched behind one of the potted plants, the long snout of his sniper rifle extending through the leaves. Chisnall lay on the ground in the middle of the passageway and trained his coil-gun on the door at the far end.

They didn't have to wait long. The door began to open, then slammed shut as Wilton's rifle cracked. The bullet ricocheted inside the dorm.

Chisnall shoved a frag canister into his grenade launcher.

The door opened a fraction and two objects dropped through. Smoke filled that end of the room.

Monster began to fire blindly into the smoke, and answering fire came immediately from invisible opponents. Chisnall raised his gun and fired the grenade launcher. He miscalculated—the grenade hit the ceiling about halfway down the dorm and exploded. He tried again, lowering the angle. This time, the explosion lit up the smoke from within.

A dark rectangular shape appeared through the swirling smoke: a door, ripped from its frame. The Pukes were using it as a shield.

"Fall back, fall back, to the school!" Chisnall yelled as the aliens surged forward. "You first, Wilton, then Monster. I'll cover you."

He emptied his clip into the smoke, then replaced it with a fresh one.

"Brogan, Price, how are you doing?"

"We're in the shaft, climbing up," Brogan answered. "One of the older kids has done this before and knows how to open the air filters. He's gone up first. But a couple of younger ones didn't want to climb into the shaft. We had to convince them."

"Price?"

"Just what she said," Price said. "Don't worry. One false move and I'll get some revenge for Hunter."

Chisnall didn't doubt it.

"Okay, keep them moving. We'll be right behind you."

Chisnall rolled sideways across the room to the passageway. He jumped to his feet and ran, reaching the school just after Monster. Wilton was already inside, covering them from the doorway. He moved aside as they ran in and then kicked the door shut.

"What now?" he asked.

"We need to slow them down. Give ourselves time to get

into the air shaft," Chisnall said. "Get the prisoners. We'll send them out. They'll have to deal with them."

Wilton disappeared to the back of the room. Chisnall opened the door a fraction to an immediate flurry of shots.

"We have hostages," he yelled. "Stop shooting."

A couple of shots seemed to disagree, but they stopped quickly when a voice that Chisnall knew sounded out loudly.

"Chizna?" Yozi called.

Chisnall turned to the others and muttered, "Does this guy ever give up?" Then he called out, "Yes."

"There's no way out. Send out the hostages."

"If I do that, you'll kill us," Chisnall said.

"Surrender, and you won't be harmed. You have my word," Yozi said.

Chisnall wasn't sure whether that was true or not, but in any case it didn't matter. They were just buying time. He shut the door.

Wilton approached with the alien scientists and other staff. He and Monster covered them with their sidearms.

"Who's in charge?" Chisnall asked.

One of the Pukes raised his head, the Bzadian equivalent of raising a hand.

"We're going to let you go," Chisnall said. "But listen to me. We have hidden a powerful bomb inside this complex. You have"—he looked at his watch—"a little more than twenty minutes to evacuate. Head for the entrance and run for your lives. If you are not out of the monorail tunnel when it explodes . . ." He let that thought sink in. Then he opened the door a crack again and called out, "Hostages are coming out now. Do not shoot."

The hostages started to surge forward, panicked by the thought of the bomb. That was exactly what Chisnall wanted. He flung the door open and stepped back. There were no shots; the Bzadian soldiers were too well disciplined for that.

The hostages massed at the doorway, pressing to get out: out of the schoolroom, out of the complex, out of Uluru.

"Okay, we are Oscar Mike," Chisnall said quietly on the comm. He tapped Monster on the arm and nodded.

It would take the Pukes a few moments to deal with the panicky group of hostages. They ran back through to the doorway at the end of the recreation area, which led to the utility passageway and into the plant room.

Wilton wedged his M110 under the handle of the door.

"Won't be needing that anymore," he said.

They found the air shaft at the rear of the plant room, a large round tube that disappeared into the rock of the wall. An inspection hatch was open on the side of it. A couple of crates were stacked below it, and Chisnall signaled for Wilton to go first. He climbed up and disappeared into the shaft.

He tried Brogan on the comm but got no answer. Hopefully she was outside the rock and out of comm range. He prayed she hadn't betrayed them again, alerting the Bzadians somehow or blocking the entrance so they'd be sealed in the shaft when the bomb went off. But if she'd done either of those things, there was nothing he could do about it now.

He climbed into the shaft on the heels of Wilton and turned back to see Monster move the crates away behind the machine, hiding them from view. Then Monster leaped and pulled himself halfway up into the shaft. Chisnall grabbed him by the collar and hauled him the rest of the way inside.

Monster pulled the hatch shut behind them.

"I don't think that will fool them for long," Chisnall said. He checked his watch. They were twenty minutes away from a massive explosion.

Yozi cursed and pushed his way through the last of the terrified scientists who were crushing through the narrow doorway.

The scumbugz were gone.

Alizza appeared beside him. "We need to evacuate," he said.

"You evacuate," Yozi said. "I'm not letting those scumbugz get away."

Yozi ran to the recreation room and scanned around, seeing no one. A doorway was located at the rear and he took it, realizing that Alizza was still at his heels.

He tried the closed door at the end of the passageway. The handle moved, then jammed. Blocked from the inside.

He kicked at the door a couple of times, but it was too solid for that.

"Out of the way," Alizza said, pulling a grenade off his belt.

An explosion sounded down below them, and Chisnall looked back.

"Keep moving," Monster said.

That was easier said than done. After the initial horizontal shaft into the wall, there was a short vertical climb with metal rungs. Then came a long, steep slope. In places, the shaft widened out enough that they could crawl on their hands and knees, and at other times it was only just wide enough to squeeze through narrow gaps. The rock walls were rough. He wondered how Monster was managing with his wide shoulders.

They reached the first air filter, a fine mesh grille that clipped to both sides of the shaft. It had been left unclipped and was leaning back against the left side. The shaft was a little wider here to accommodate the size of the filter. Monster reached down and clipped it back into place after he passed through.

Eighteen minutes.

It was Alizza who spotted the hatch on the shaft leading into the huge air pump. Two bolts that should have held it shut were hanging loosely. He flung the hatch open with a metallic clang and gave Yozi a foot up into the shaft. Then Yozi reached back down and helped Alizza up.

There were sounds ahead of them. Sounds of scuffling, scrabbling hands and feet, echoing through the narrow tunnel back to them.

Yozi wasted no time, propelling himself forward with Alizza close behind. They climbed the rungs in the vertical section two at a time and stopped only when a dark barrier blocked the way. Yozi risked a flash of his utility light. An air filter. Clips at all four corners held it in place.

Yozi unclipped three of the clips when the filter slipped from his grasp and clanged to the floor.

The sound of the filter falling was like an alarm bell to Chisnall.

Someone was coming up the shaft behind them. How close were they? Chisnall wasn't waiting around to find out. He could see light ahead of them, a glowing hole that grew larger as he approached the end of the shaft.

Then he was out, grabbing at the rocky edge and hauling himself onto the red rock of Uluru. He was on top of the rock—no, not quite. Sloping, rocky walls hemmed him in on three sides. He was in a huge cleft in the top of Uluru. The air shaft behind him was just a hole in the rock, protected from the elements by a hood and a metal grille that now lay on the ground. Some scrubby trees stuck at awkward angles out of boulders in a river at the base of the cleft.

A river?

That was when he realized it was raining. The rain was constant and heavy, with huge droplets that exploded off his visor. Gushing water ran down the slope, disappearing around a sharp corner in the rock. It seemed incongruous, here on the top of this normally dry red rock.

The children were sitting in a group, holding on to each other, huddled against the rain on the flattest part of the slope. Brogan sat with them, playing a simple hand game with two of the younger ones. Price stood behind Brogan, covering her with her sidearm without making it obvious. Wilton was starting to climb up the rocky face of the cleft, no doubt to get a better view of what was around them. Price held up the transmitter when she saw Chisnall.

"I've been pressing it for ten minutes and nothing," she said.

He looked up, suddenly worried. Could the walls be blocking the signal? He examined the cleft. Could they climb up with the transmitter? How long would that take?

"Press it again," he said, but there was no need.

From the top of the rock, a dark shape emerged. It was a Bzadian rotorcraft, a giant metal umbrella giving them brief respite from the rain, although the downwash of the blades bent back the trees and threatened to blow them all from their precarious perch. Then it passed over and dropped down, lower and lower. The markings on the side of the craft came into view: a giant red cross. A medivac rotorcraft.

It nudged closer and closer until the edge of the outer ring was touching the rock.

"Wait here," Chisnall yelled over the roar of the machine.

He scrambled down the cleft to the rotorcraft and leaped from the rock onto the slipway over the blades, running up and into the craft itself.

The two pilots, humans, looked around as he stuck his head up into the cockpit.

"I'm Chisnall," he said.

"What's with all the kids?" one of them asked. "We came to pick up eight soldiers, not a freaking school trip."

"Change of plans," Chisnall said. "We need to take them all."

"Can't take that many," said the copilot. "These things only hold about fifteen people; there must be forty of them."

"They're little," Chisnall said.

"I won't get lift," the pilot said. "Not with all of you."

"Then just take the kids," Chisnall said. "And this one." He pointed to Brogan. "Lock the cockpit door and don't let her in under any circumstances. She's a traitor and dangerous."

"That's still too many—" the copilot began, but the pilot cut him off.

"We'll try," he said. "What about you?"

"We'll find our own way out of here," Chisnall said.

The pilot shook his head as if he thought Chisnall was crazy. "We've got a backup rotorcraft waiting over at Lake Amadeus. Wait here, and I'll get them to pick you up."

"There's no time," Chisnall said. "It's only minutes before that warhead explodes. We'll try and get clear of the rock first."

"Okay. I'll let them know to come for you."

"Understood," Chisnall said. He ran quickly back down the slipway to the rock. The edge of the craft dipped slightly as he stepped carefully off onto the damp, slippery rock.

"Get them on board," he said. "Just Brogan and the kids. The rest of us are going to have to find our own way home."

"What the hell?" Wilton said. "She killed Hunter, and she gets a free ride home?"

"The rotorcraft can't take us all," Chisnall said. "If we've got any shot of getting out of here alive, it won't be with dragging Brogan along."

"Easily solved," Price said. "Just throw her off the edge of the rock. Then there's one more place on the rotorcraft."

"And who gets that?" Chisnall asked. "You?"

Price looked at him steadily for a moment, then looked away.

Chisnall pointed to the transmitter that Price was holding. "They know everything. She'll be put on trial. And who knows, maybe they'll get information out of her that can help win this damn war."

"And we're still expendable, right?" Price said.

"Yes, but we're not expended yet," Chisnall said.

20. FOOLS RUSH

THEY WATCHED THE CRAFT DEPART, OVERLOADED AND struggling to gain lift. It almost didn't make it. Tipping and tilting dangerously toward the rock face, the craft somehow found its wings and clawed its way into the air.

To any aliens who saw it, or any Bzadian radar stations that were still operational, it was just one of their own hospital ships. There were dozens of them buzzing over the base since the air raid. Even if they suspected it, what would they do—shoot down one of their own medical craft?

Hovering off the northwestern coast of Australia was a huge task force. Massed ships and squadrons of planes waiting, circling, providing an umbrella of safety. If the rotorcraft could reach that umbrella, it would be safe.

Monster stood at the entrance to the shaft, his sidearm trained on the black hole that led back down into the rock.

He tapped an ear and pointed into the shaft. He could hear their pursuers. They must be close.

"Okay, we're Oscar Mike," Chisnall said, stepping carefully to avoid the steadily rising watercourse.

He looked around. Up or down? *Down,* he thought. He didn't know what a China Lake warhead plus a room full of fuel cells would do to the big rock, and he didn't want to stick around to find out. He peered down the steep slope and took a step down the cleft, looking for a safe way to descend, away from the torrent of water the stream had now become.

His foot slipped and he went down hard, sliding down the wet slope toward the water. He grabbed at one of the trees to stop himself, but the branch cracked and gave way, and suddenly he was in a raging, whitewater deluge, heading full throttle toward the edge of the cliff.

Price reached out as he passed, grabbing at his arm, but there was no way she could hold him and her fingers slipped on his wet armor. The water twisted him around just in time to see her overbalance. Wilton reached out to help, and then they were both in the water as well.

It was not a smooth ride. Boulders and scrub hammered and clawed at him as the edge of the rock approached. Then suddenly the watercourse swept around to the left, away from the cliff's edge, dumping him into a much faster river that flowed down the deep scar across Uluru.

He went under, struggling for air, then popped back to the surface as the watercourse widened and the water shallowed. Beneath him was a bed of scraggly rocks, and he was sure he hit each one, arms and legs flailing, as the water surged down.

Then the canyon narrowed again, the water deepening and the speed increasing. The slope was much steeper here. He made another sharp turn to the left and in front of him he saw certain death: a clump of massive boulders. The water was hitting the boulders at full force, smashing and spraying up into the air, then over and around them.

He braced himself for the impact.

The first boulder rose up above him, but a giant hand from below seemed to lift him as the water surged up and over. His boots scraped the top of the boulder; then he flew through the air and splashed back down into a torrent on the other side. He kept his head above water long enough to look back and see Price flying over the same boulder with Wilton right behind her, arms windmilling through the air.

Finally the ride became smooth, like a waterslide at a fun park, and steeper again. A sharp turn to the left, a sweeping curve to the right. He saw the ground approach, a pool of darkness in the shadow of the cleft in the side of the rock. Then with a whoosh and a roar of bubbles he was underwater—deep underwater—and sinking.

He tried to swim up to the surface, but it was impossible in his heavy armor and boots. His outstretched arm connected with a rock on the edge of the pool, and he dragged himself forward underwater, his lungs screaming. He felt a shock as a large object exploded into the water beside him—Price.

Chisnall reached over and grabbed her, pulling her along with him.

Another surge of water as another body hit the deep pool, and then another.

His hand closed on a metal bar, and he used it to pull himself up. Then he found another bar, a metal railing out of the water. He looped an elbow around it and pulled Price up beside him. She coughed, choked, and vomited water, but her other hand had a steely grip on Wilton's collar and a moment later he, too, was grasping the metal railing, gasping, choking, but alive.

"Monster?" Chisnall called out.

"Here," came a voice that he could not have been happier to hear.

He turned and saw the big Hungarian clinging to a rock on the far side of the pool.

"You fall in too?" Chisnall grinned.

"Fall in? My dude! The Monster jumped in," Monster managed, gasping in air. "You guys looked like you were having so much fun."

"Anybody break anything?" Chisnall asked.

"All Oscar Kilo," Wilton said.

"I think I sprained my wrist," Price said. "I'll be fine."

"The Monster thinks he sprained his arse," Monster said. "But he can walk."

"Let's get out of here," Chisnall said. "Try and put some distance between us and this rock before those Pukes in the air shaft catch up with us."

"Where the hell are we?" Wilton asked.

"The rock pool at Mutitjulu," Chisnall said. "We're not far from the main entrance, if I remember the geography of Uluru correctly. How long have we got before the warhead blows?"

"Don't know," Monster said.

Chisnall swung a leg over the railing and waded through the knee-deep water on the other side. It became more and more shallow until he was on a concrete path. Before the Pukes came, this was the trail that had brought tourists to the rock pool. They had been clinging to the tourists' safety fence. Now the whole lot was underwater, and judging by the surging water that flowed down from the side of the rock, it was going to get deeper quickly.

He stared for a moment at the raging waters above his head, finding it hard to comprehend that the four of them had come down that and survived.

Price was holding her sprained arm with her other hand. He stopped.

"Let me look at that," he said.

"I'm Oscar Kilo," she said with a gritted smile.

He ignored her and took her arm. Her wrist hung limply and at an odd angle.

"Sprained? Like hell," Chisnall said. "It's broken."

That was the hand he had hauled her out of the pool with, but she hadn't screamed, hadn't complained at all.

"We've got bigger things to worry about than my wrist," Price said, looking back at the rock.

It was hard to disagree with that.

"Rip off your bomb squad markings," he said, and helped Price with hers.

Ahead of him, through the thundering rain, Chisnall could see the sweeping curve of the monorail track heading left, back toward the entrance of the rock. The concrete path they were standing on came to a fork, one branch leading back toward the entrance and the other heading out among the buildings and streets of the Bzadian base.

The last place he wanted to be when the warhead went off was near that entrance. But he changed his mind as a dark shape caught his eye.

"This way," he said, heading to the left.

"Are you sure, LT?" Monster asked.

"Look," Chisnall said, pointing.

Through the high-security fence that blocked off access to the tunnel buildings, they could see the abandoned battle tank, its main gun shattered. It sat next to the remains of the Uluru entrance building, a jumble of stone blocks. Beyond it, a huge, wheeled crane had just lowered the edge of the second battle tank to the ground. The tank that had capsized earlier. The tank's crew stood around it, waiting for the crane to unhook.

The Angel Team got to the fence and skirted around the outside to the gaping hole where the tanks had originally busted their way through.

A technician climbed out of an access panel of the first tank as they approached.

"How is it?" Chisnall asked, as if he had every right to be there.

The technician looked around, protecting his eyes from the rain with his hand. If he was surprised at the sight of the four bedraggled soldiers, he didn't show it. Everybody was soaking wet anyway, Chisnall realized, from the thunderstorm.

"It'll be pretty shaken up in there," the worker said, "and the main gun is out, but I got the electrics working again. Are you the maintenance crew?"

"Yes," Chisnall replied.

"They said you wouldn't be here until tomorrow," the worker said. "I'll have to get clearance from my supervisor. Apparently there's a group of terrorists running around."

"There is," Chisnall agreed. "They're in there." He pointed to the rock. "And the whole rock is about to explode. Haven't you been given evacuation orders?"

The worker looked frightened. "Evacuation? No. Nothing!"

"Get moving, now! We'll see if we can get this tank to safety. Go!"

Chisnall didn't wait for an answer. He ducked underneath the metal rim of the tank, the others right behind him.

"You need to wait for clearance," the worker said behind him. "Hey!"

Chisnall ignored him. The entrance hatch was open, and he clambered up into it, reaching back and giving Price a hand so that she could avoid putting weight on her wrist.

Only a dim glow from an emergency light lit the interior.

They were in a kind of well, a circular depression in the base of the tank. A short ladder led up to the control center.

They climbed the ladder and found two sets of controls on one side that were clearly for steering the tank, while two on the other side were for the weapons systems.

"Hey!" Chisnall heard again from outside, but it was cut off by a metallic clang as he found a lever on the control panel that slid the hatch shut.

Chisnall slid into the driver's seat. It was large and padded. Surprisingly comfortable. It occurred to him that the padding might be protection against the shock of explosions outside the hull rather than a creature comfort.

The rain was a muted thrum on the outer shell of the tank.

Price slid into the seat next to him. That would be for the tank commander, or possibly a navigator. Maybe a communications officer.

The desk in front of him was covered with lights, buttons, readouts, and switches. It looked like the control panel of a jetliner.

Price put something down on the desk, and a dim, red flash caught Chisnall's eye. The transmitter. Somehow she had managed to hang on to it throughout the wild slide down the rock and the plunge into the pool. All with just one good arm.

"Better leave this running," Price said. "Otherwise our rotorcraft ride home is likely to bug out at the sight of a Bzadian battle tank."

"True," Chisnall said. "Now let's see if we can work out how to drive this thing."

Price moved her good hand and pressed a switch. The interior cabin filled with light. Screens lit up around them. There were no windows, Chisnall realized. No grilles. No way of looking out. That couldn't be right. They had to see where they were going.

A helmet hung on a hook to the right of the desk. A thick wire protruded from the base of it. He put it on and a visor flicked down over his eyes. Suddenly he was looking outside the tank. Images from cameras embedded in the hulls were projected in front of his eyes. If he turned his head, the view moved. He twisted around and found he was looking directly behind the tank. He had full 360-degree vision, yet he was securely encased inside the machine.

Somehow the control panel in front of him was still visible, a ghostly image that seemed to be superimposed on the world outside. He turned toward Price and could see her reasonably clearly. He found that if he focused his eyes on the outside world, it became clear, and if he focused on the inside of the tank, it moved into sharp focus. He wasn't sure if it was his eyes doing that or some clever trick of the helmet software. Price was putting on a helmet of her own.

"Wilton, Monster, get on the gunnery controls," Chisnall said.

"The gun is out," Wilton said. "Thanks to Monster."

"Some people are never happy," Monster said.

"See what other armaments there are," Chisnall said.

Price found a starter button, and the machine shuddered into life before settling down into a smooth purr that smothered the sound of the rain. Chisnall examined the rest of the controls. Moving the tank seemed simple. It was controlled by two palm-sized knobs. He turned the knob on the left and the tank slowly rumbled forward, toward Uluru. The other one must be for speed.

"Wrong way," he muttered, and eased the right-hand knob around. As he did, there was a feeling of movement, and he realized that the cabin had rotated inside the tank, automatically orienting itself to the direction of travel.

The controls made human vehicles—with their gas pedals, brakes, steering wheels, and forward and reverse gears—seem hopelessly complicated. One knob for speed. The other for direction. The tank could move in any direction. So to go in reverse, he would simply turn the right-hand knob in that direction.

"And now we just roll on out of here," Wilton said.

"It's that simple," Chisnall said, not quite believing it.

"It's *not* that simple," Price said.

He turned to look where she was looking.

"I don't believe it," he said.

Yozi, indestructible Yozi, and the big soldier, Alizza, were running toward them, weapons in hand.

"Time we got moving," Chisnall said, and spun both knobs.

The machine surged forward, heading right for Yozi.

Chisnall kept it on course for a moment, watching Yozi

and Alizza throw themselves to the side, out of the path of the raging tank. A fence in front of them was quickly gone, trampled under the huge ball wheels of the tank. Then he steered the tank back onto the approach road. The road led into the city, and from there they could find their way north.

"This is madness. We'll never make it," Price said.

"Doesn't stop us trying," Chisnall said.

He glanced around and saw Yozi and Alizza running toward the other tank, yelling at the tank crew. The crew scrambled inside. Now the other tank was accelerating.

"How are those guns coming?" Chisnall asked calmly.

"I think we found the fire button," Monster said.

"You're gonna need it," Chisnall said. He twisted the speed knob around as far as it would go and the tank charged toward the low outer fence line.

Price was studying the controls. She pressed a large red button, and around them the hull of the tank began to vibrate. It started as a hum, then became a high-pitched whine as the hull started spinning.

The outer fence line was rapidly approaching. In just a few meters, they could lose themselves between the big stone buildings beyond it. But a quick glance back showed the gun turret of the second tank was coming around to aim at them.

"Incoming!" he yelled.

There was a flash from the other tank's gun, then a clang on the outer hull, followed by an explosion from one of the buildings. Smoke and dust billowed around them.

"What the hell?" Wilton asked.

"Takes a direct hit to kill one of these things," Chisnall said. "Anything else ricochets off."

They had made it between the buildings, racing down the narrow street, away from Uluru, out of sight of the following tank—for the moment, at least.

Chisnall gritted his teeth and steered around a tight corner to the right, to the north, toward the base boundary and the desert beyond. They almost didn't make it. The outer edge of the huge tank gouged a long scar along one of the buildings, but then they straightened, and Chisnall twisted the speed knob back to maximum. Full speed ahead.

A Land Rover was parked to one side. He ignored it and felt the tank rise up slightly as it rolled over the top, crushing it.

A truck turned a corner and approached them head-on. The street was not wide enough for them both. The truck swerved madly from side to side, then smoked poured from its brakes. The driver burst out the door, fell, and rolled in the street before jumping up and running to flatten himself against a building.

The tank hit the truck off center and carried it down the road for ten or twenty meters before the back of the truck slipped sideways, striking one of the buildings and wedging there. The chassis was crushed and the cab exploded in flames.

"I got twin heavy coil-guns," Wilton said. "Locked and loaded."

Machine guns wouldn't do much against a battle tank, but it was better than nothing.

"Aim for the barrel," Chisnall said. "That worked once before."

Chisnall felt the weight of the tank shift slightly as the turret and the mangled barrel of the tank's main gun rotated around to the rear.

There was a thundering sound as the second tank turned the corner and appeared behind them. In the video visor, Chisnall saw Wilton's tracer rounds spark off it.

The other tank fired. There was another clang from the hull and a building shattered and collapsed in the street behind them. Their pursuers had to slow as the tank climbed over the jagged rock in its path.

That gave Chisnall an idea.

He spun the tank wide around another corner, another tight side street. He deliberately let the tank climb up onto the sidewalk and into the curved stone side of a tall, thin building. Stone exploded in every direction; then they were past. The building, robbed of its base, tottered for a moment, then toppled, huge chunks of rock completely blocking the street.

The second tank appeared, smashing through some of the rubble before slowly clambering up over the rest. As the front of it rose up, Wilton hit them with the heavy coil-guns, hoping to strike the more delicate underside of the tank.

"Damn," he said as the rounds just bounced off.

Chisnall turned and turned again, hoping to lose their pursuers in the maze of side streets.

He continued to head north, toward the outer barrier, the

lake, and their only hope of salvation. Cars and jeeps disappeared under the massive ball wheels of the juggernaut. Fuel tanks exploded, jarring the tank but not damaging it in the slightest.

The other tank appeared on a parallel road, visible down a side street.

"To your left!" Chisnall yelled.

The turret rotated, but they were already past the intersection, and the other tank was hidden behind tall buildings.

They were almost to the outer perimeter wall when the second tank appeared behind them, firing. Another, much heavier clang from the hull told Chisnall that their enemy was finding its range. There was a sudden plume of dirt out in the desert as the shell ricocheted off and exploded, although the rain quickly washed it out of the sky.

They smashed through the low boundary wall, the tank juddering over the crushed remains.

The going was faster over the flat, open desert, but here there was nothing to hide behind. Chisnall veered the big machine from side to side, not wanting to give Yozi an easy, steady shot.

Wilton fired continuously but had no effect on the thick, spinning metal of the other battle tank.

But the enemy tank did not return the fire.

"Fast movers, eight o'clock," Price said, her eyes on a radar screen. "Two of them."

Chisnall glanced to the left. Two type ones, screaming in from the west, below the heavy rainclouds. Death from the sky. No tank hull could survive a direct hit from a Bzadian jet's missile.

"LT!" Price yelled, pulling his attention back to the front.

Before them, rising out of the desert, was the ugly, multi-pronged shape of a Bzadian gunship. It was a three-sided attack, Chisnall saw, and there was no way out. Behind them, the tank; in front, the gunship; and high in the sky, silhouetted above Uluru, the two alien jets.

There was no chance to escape. No hope left. And no panic. He felt calm, perhaps because of the sheer hopelessness of the situation. Death was coming fast, and there was absolutely nothing he could do about it.

"Been a good effort, team," he said.

That was when Uluru began to dance.

It shuddered, as if terribly afraid, and fire burst out of the side of the rock, through the tunnel entrance. Another shaft of fire, like a man-made bolt of lightning, appeared at the top of the rock, in the cleft—the ventilation shaft. It was so powerful that even the clouds parted around it.

The entire top of Uluru seemed to rise up, as if drawing in a breath. Then the rock exhaled through the monorail tunnel, and all hell came with it. A billowing, fiery shock wave punched straight through the base behind them.

Buildings, vehicles, everything in its path, disappeared into the cloud of dust.

Even out in the desert, well out of the cone of destruction, inside a solid metal battle tank, Chisnall felt the force of the explosive anger.

Behind them, the second tank, closer to the outer edge of the blast, rocked on its suspension. Two figures on the back of the tank went flying, arms and legs cartwheeling through the air, slamming into the wet sand of the desert.

In front of them, the gunship rotorcraft shook and shimmied in the sky but held its position.

The fast movers were not so lucky. They were almost directly over Uluru when it blew. The upward blast of burning fuel hit one of the jets, spinning it like a football. It rolled sideways, clipping the tail of the other jet. For a second, it looked as though they would both recover. Then the first jet exploded, dissolving in a fireball, while the second, without a tail, spiraled into the desert.

Chisnall stared at the fire and dust pouring out through the openings in Uluru. The tank's cameras saw the explosion, but his mind saw more. Much more. He saw the faces of the young mothers, impaled on their cots by snaking tubes, their dull eyes reflecting the white flare of the blast for a fraction of a second before they vanished forever.

The jets were gone, but it wasn't over yet. In front of them, flashes came from the gunship. Rockets.

Chisnall shut his eyes, waiting for the impact.

"They're firing too high!" Price yelled.

He opened his eyes and looked up to see the trails of the rockets passing over their heads—two of them. He twisted around and saw a brilliant flash as they both impacted, dead center, on the tank behind them. It exploded with a brilliant flash and a scream of rent metal, jagged hunks of tank rising in parabolic arcs before crashing down into the desert sand.

"They got the wrong tank!" Wilton yelled. "They got the wrong tank!"

"No, they didn't," Chisnall said.

He watched the rotorcraft sink to the ground in front of them. The transmitter on the tank's desk continued to flash, identifying them. The pilot of the medivac craft had said a second craft would be coming for them. He had just neglected to say that that craft would be a gunship.

Chisnall turned the knob gently and rolled the big tank forward, pulling it to a halt just in front of the rotorcraft.

"We are Oscar Mike," he said, jumping down into the well. "We are Oscar freaking Mike."

As they ran across the open desert to the waiting rotorcraft, Chisnall glanced back at the burning hulk of the second tank.

Behind it, in the sand of the desert, he could see two crawling figures. Yozi and Alizza. He flicked a salute at them as he ran up onto the gunship. They'd never see it. But it felt like the right thing to do.

Exhausted, Chisnall collapsed into a seat in the small, circular bay in the interior of the gunship. Price sat next to him, supporting her broken wrist on her knee. She barely seemed to notice it. Her head was down, staring at the floor.

There were no other seats, so Wilton and Monster propped

themselves up against the curved wall of the bay. Wilton closed his eyes, but Monster stared at Chisnall, grinning.

"The Monster thinks that was better than a really good fart, my dudes."

Wilton groaned. Chisnall laughed. Price was silent.

He thought about Hunter, resting forever in the sands of the desert.

He thought about Brogan. His now ex-girlfriend. Had she ever had feelings for him? Or was that all just part of her plan? Probably he would never know. And for Brogan, Chisnall knew, the relief at surviving would be tempered by the knowledge of what would be waiting for her back in the Free Territories.

As the rotorcraft took off, Chisnall looked back at Uluru and the triangular path of destruction centered on the monorail entrance. Flames were still belching from the air shaft, and a cloud of gray dust hung around the top of the rock. It slowly disappeared behind them, first a lump of rock, then a pebble, then a dot on the landscape. Then it was gone, swallowed by the vastness of the Australian desert.

END NOTE

THERE ARE VARYING ACCOUNTS OF MANY OF THE EVENTS on the Uluru mission. But the key facts are not in question, only some of the finer details.

For example, some historians have claimed that Lieutenant Ryan Chisnall did not fall into the watercourse down the side of Uluru, but rather jumped into it willingly, knowing that it would end up in the rock pool at Mutitjulu. The most reliable account of this particular event, however, comes from Captain Trianne Price, ACOG, Recon Team Angel (Ret.). She states that, in her opinion, Chisnall simply slipped, and that if it was a planned move, he would have said something to the others first.

Price was awarded the Victoria Cross (by the New Zealand government) and the Bzadian War Medal (by the New Earth Council) for her courage in laying the explosives on the monorail track in the face of the approaching car.

There are also varying stories about the role of Specialist Janos Panyoczki (Monster). Historian Hayden Glanville, in his study of the Uluru mission, came to the conclusion that Monster was there to keep an eye on Chisnall. Not even the team commander was above suspicion. Panyoczki, still on active duty, is now a general in the Hungarian Free Army. He has never consented to any interviews about his service during the Bzadian War, so it is unlikely that these questions will ever be answered.

At his parents' request, the grave of Specialist Stephen Huntington was located after the end of the war, although no remains were found.

Specialist Blake Wilton continued to serve with both the Angel and Demon Recon teams, before he grew too tall for undercover missions and transferred to the Canadian Land Force Command. He served with honor and distinction, earning the Medal of Military Valour and two Sacrifice Medals before losing his life heroically in the Battle of Bering Strait during the Second Great Ice War.

Staff Sergeant Holly Brogan received a pardon from the New Earth Council after agreeing to assist in locating other Uluru children who had already infiltrated human society. She passed on extensive inside knowledge of the Bzadian military, which helped bring about a turning point in the war. She is now considered a national hero of Australia.

Lieutenant Ryan Chisnall returned to alien-occupied territory with other members of Recon Team Angel less than six months later, as part of Operation Magnum. They got out. He did not. An emergency signal was picked up by satellite, but an extraction team found no trace of Chisnall. Official reports list him as missing, presumed killed, in action.

His luck, it seems, had finally run out.

GLOSSARY

Everything about the Allied Combined Operations Group (ACOG) was a mishmash of different human cultures: tactics, weapons, languages, vehicles, and especially terminology. The success of many missions depended on troops from diverse nations being able to understand all communications instantly and thoroughly. The establishment of a Standardized Military Terminology and Phonetic Alphabet (SMTPA) was a key factor in assisting this communication, combining existing terminology from many of the countries involved in ACOG. For ease of understanding, here is a short glossary of some of the SMTPA terms, phonetic shortcuts, and equipment used in this book.

Air mobile: airborne vehicle

Bogie: enemy aircraft

Cal: caliber (of weapon)

Chaff: metallic strips dropped in a cloud to confuse enemy radar

Claymore mine: directional antipersonnel mine

Clear copy: "Your transmission is clear."

Coil-gun: weapon using magnetic coils to propel a projectile

Comm: personal radio communicator

EV (Echo Victor): exit vehicle

FACC-E: free-fall air-cushioned container—equipment

Fast mover: fixed-wing aircraft such as a jet fighter

Foot mobile: person walking

GPS: global positioning system

Ground mobile: land-based vehicle, such as a car or truck

HAFLP-P (Half-pipe): high-altitude free-fall landing pad—personnel

HMDS: helmet-mounted display system

How copy: "Is my transmission clear?"

Klick: kilometer

LAV: light armored vehicle

LT: lieutenant

Mike: minute

NV goggles: night-vision goggles

Oscar Kilo: okay

Oscar Mike: on the move

PFC: private first class

Puke: military slang for a Bzadian.

Rotorcraft: helicopter with internal rotor blades at the base of the craft

RV: rendezvous point

SAM: surface-to-air missile

Sit rep: situation report

Slow mover: rotary-wing aircraft such as a helicopter or rotorcraft

Spec: specialist

Sys-check: systems check

Sys-OK: systems check completed okay

Tab: hike or walk

Three, six, etc.: direction given as per a clock face

NOTE ON PRONUNCIATION

There is no equivalent in English for the buzzing sound that is a common feature of most Bzadian languages. As per convention, this sound is represented, where required, with the letter *z*.

NOTE ON BZADIAN ARMY RANKS

The ranking system and unit structure of the Bzadian Army are markedly different from those of most Earth forces. Many ranks have no equivalent in human terms, and the organization of units is different. For simplicity and ease of understanding, the closest human rank has been used when referring to Bzadian Army ranks, and Bzadian unit names have been expressed in human terms.

CONGRATULATIONS

The following people won the grand prize in my school competitions and have all had a character named after them in this book:

Theo Bennett

Hebron Christian College, Auckland, New Zealand

Conna Brajkovich

Sir Edmund Hillary Library, Auckland, New Zealand

Holly Brogan

St. Cuthberts College, Auckland, New Zealand

Bryan Brown

Vista Del Valle School, Los Angeles, USA

Easton Bunker

Alexander Dawson School, Las Vegas, USA

Ryan Chisnall

Belmont Intermediate, Auckland, New Zealand

Sean Fleming

Masterton Intermediate, Masterton, New Zealand

Hayden Glanville

St. Patricks at Strathfield, New South Wales, Australia

Bonnie Kelaart

Lowood State School, Queensland, Australia

Janos Panyoczki

Kaiwaka School, Kaiwaka, New Zealand

Trianne Price

Woodcrest State College, Queensland, Australia

Blake Wilton

Orewa College, Orewa, New Zealand

ACKNOWLEDGMENTS

Anyone who has ever published a book will tell you about the debt they owe to the books they read in their formative years. For me, it was the adventure thrillers of Alistair MacLean. Recon Team Angel is in many ways a tribute to books like *Where Eagles Dare* and *The Guns of Navarone.*

I stand on the shoulders of giants.

ABOUT THE AUTHOR

A native New Zealander, **BRIAN FALKNER** now lives on the other side of the Tasman Sea, in Australia. To research the settings for *The Assault,* he camped in the Australian Outback, sleeping under the stars and visiting Uluru. Find him online at brianfalkner.com.